ON TRACK FOR TERROR

Joe took off in pursuit of the man who had nearly pushed Callie onto the tracks. The guy darted to the edge of the subway platform, trying to wriggle through the crowd.

It didn't work. Joe stretched out an arm and caught him by the shoulder, turning him around.

The man quickly took his hand out of his pocket, clenched in a fist. Joe moved, ready to block a blow, but this guy wasn't throwing a punch. Instead his hand opened about a foot from Joe's face, releasing a cloud of reddish powder that burned Joe's eyes as if someone had thrown acid in them.

Suddenly blinded, Joe recoiled. His antagonist gave him a vicious shove, and Joe staggered backward, his arms flailing. His right foot stepped back and found only air under it.

Joe was going over the edge of the platform— just as the train was coming in!

Books in THE HARDY BOYS CASEFILES™ Series

Available from ARCHWAY Paperbacks

DIPLOMATIC DECEIT

FRANKLIN W. DIXON

AN ARCHWAY PAPERBACK
Published by POCKET BOOKS
New York   London   Toronto   Sydney   Tokyo   Singapore

AN ARCHWAY PAPERBACK *Original*

An Archway Paperback published by
POCKET BOOKS, a division of Simon & Schuster Inc.
1230 Avenue of the Americas, New York, NY 10020

ISBN: 0-671-67486-2

First Archway Paperback printing April 1990

10 9 8 7 6 5 4 3 2 1

Printed in the U.S.A.

IL 7+

DIPLOMATIC DECEIT

Chapter
1

"Do you think we should get out of the cab in case Callie explodes?" Joe Hardy's blue eyes danced with laughter as he leaned forward in his seat to see past Callie Shaw. He wanted to hear what his brother on the other side of the cab was going to say.

Frank Hardy gave his kid brother a grin and slipped an arm around his girlfriend, Callie, who was between them. "Oh, I don't think she's ready to explode," he said in a low, teasing voice. "Not yet, at least."

Callie threw out her arms, shaking her head so her blond hair flew around her head. "Okay, so I'm excited—why not? I've been thinking about nothing but this trip for three weeks now, ever since Madeleine and her family came to America."

"Tell me about it," Joe said sarcastically.

Callie ignored the remark. "When you've got a foreign pen pal, you don't expect to meet him or her. I knew from Maddy's letters that her father was a French diplomat, but I never expected him to come to Washington. Now I can actually meet my friend, after swapping letters all these years."

Joe rolled his eyes. "So, Frank, did you know about this mysterious correspondence? Maybe Callie has other pen pals, like a handsome Swede or a soulful Slav with dark gypsy eyes."

Frank Hardy stretched his six-foot-one frame. "Well, Callie? Have you been two-timing me through the international mail?" The twinkle in his dark eyes showed he was only kidding.

Callie batted her eyelashes playfully. "I'll never tell."

The cab made its way along the parkway from National Airport to the city of Washington. As they passed the military cemetery at Arlington, Virginia, they admired the bright spring flowers planted in front of the white stone gateposts. The beautiful landmark meant they were close to the bridge that crossed the Potomac River, separating Virginia from the capital city.

"This is the way I always think of Washington—everything white and classical," Frank said as they pulled onto the bridge. Even the bridge's safety rail was held up by little white concrete pillars. The joggers and bike riders who swarmed over the bridge, however, weren't dressed in white Roman togas.

Callie couldn't concentrate on the local scenery. She was much too excited. "I've been writing to Maddy Berot since I was thirteen. She's like a close friend and now I'm finally going to meet her."

"How are you going to recognize her?" Joe asked.

"I've got a recent picture in here." Callie began digging through her purse. "Maddy asked me to bring all her old letters. She's kept all of mine. We thought we'd go through them and have some laughs." She kept rummaging through a thick bundle of papers. "Here it is."

She held up a snapshot of a girl with short dark hair whose smile seemed to leap off the photograph.

Joe leaned forward for a better look. "Hey, she's pretty," he said. "I'm beginning to feel a lot better about this trip."

Frank shook his head. "You know, Callie, you could have saved us a whole lot of kicking and screaming from little brother here. All you had to do was show him that picture when you first asked him to come with us."

"You mean he didn't want to tag along?" Callie spoke with just a bit too much innocence in her voice. "I thought the world-famous Hardy Boys did everything together."

"Not exactly *everything*." Frank winked at her.

"Just when it comes to crime," Joe cut in. The Hardys actually did have a reputation for cracking mysteries and tackling tough crimes. But both Frank and Joe were happy for a rest after their last adventure, *Danger Zone*. Crime fighting had come a little too close to home when they'd had to rescue their own mother from kidnappers. They were determined that this trip should be just for fun.

Joe took the photo of Callie's pen pal and studied it. "If Maddy was a crook, I guess I could force myself to romance her to get the necessary information—"

"Yeah, yeah." Callie shook her head.

Joe put a hand on his chest. "Come on, Callie, *I'm* the one who's doing you a favor. I'm being a nice guy and going out with Maddy—"

"I'll tell you right now, Joe Hardy, I've warned Maddy about you." Callie waved a finger in his face.

Turning to his brother, Joe just raised his eyebrows. "Hear that, Frank? Callie wrote Maddy and warned her about me. I wonder what those letters say about you?"

Callie stuffed the photo and letters back in her purse. "You'll never find out," she told them.

"Maddy and I will go over these later—when we're *alone*."

She gave both the Hardys a suspicious look. "In fact, I'm going to leave these letters with Maddy—just so some people won't get the bright idea of snooping in my hotel room. I know how clever you guys are with locks and things."

Joe fell back against the seat with a pained expression on his face. "I'm shocked and hurt that you'd think Frank is capable of doing such a thing," he said, shaking his head.

"I wasn't thinking about Frank," Callie told him.

Pretending to be offended, Joe drew himself up. "Well, I hope Maddy will be nicer to me than you are, but I don't know if she will if you've been poisoning her mind against me."

"Well, we're here," Callie announced as they passed under the portico of the hotel. It was one of the glistening new brick-and-concrete buildings in the city's northwestern corner. She glanced at her watch. "We should have lots of time to check in and unpack before we head for Maddy's apartment."

"A brilliant young Frenchwoman," Joe said. "I can feel myself losing my heart already."

"Well, it may work out—as long as you don't open your mouth," Callie said, a serious note in her voice.

The doorman rescued Joe by opening the cab

door just then. "I'll take care of the bags," Joe said. "You guys go on in and register." Before he got out of the cab, he turned to Callie. "I don't suppose you have anything else you'd like to leave with me—those heavy letters, for instance?"

Callie laughed. "Keep dreaming."

A few minutes later the Hardys were in their room, checked in and unpacking their bags. "Another episode of the Joe and Callie Show," Frank said, shaking his head. "You know, you guys argue like an old married couple."

"I thought we were kidding around," Joe answered, dumping his socks and underwear into a drawer. "Jealous of all the attention Callie pays me?" He grinned. "No worries there. I've got a date with a beautiful French girl. What do you say we enjoy this visit to Washington? It should be a lot better than the last time we were down here."

Frank nodded. "Quieter, at least." The last time they'd been in Washington, they were attending a counterterrorism seminar. Callie had been involved in a hijacking and had nearly gotten killed before the boys figured out how to get onto the plane to rescue her.

"You're right, Joe," he said. "This time around, all we have to worry about is you—and whether you make a fool of yourself over Madeleine Berot." They headed out the door and down

6

the hall to the elevator. "I wonder if Monsieur Berot is here for the exhibit of the Lafayette sword."

"I didn't know he was into fencing," Joe said.

Frank couldn't believe Joe hadn't heard of the Lafayette sword. "It's an artifact that belongs to the French government. I read about it in the *Bayport Times*. At the lowest point in the American Revolutionary War, a young French nobleman, the Marquis de Lafayette, came here to help the Americans win. Grateful officers from the Continental Army presented him with a sword with a jeweled hilt or handle."

"Valuable, huh?" Joe said as they rode down in the elevator.

"Not just for the gold and jewels," Frank said. "The blade was personally inscribed by George Washington."

The elevator stopped, and they stepped out to find Callie waiting for them in the lobby.

"Ready to go?" She slid her purse strap up onto her shoulder and led the way to the door. "The Berots' place is close enough for us to walk."

Moving from the air-conditioned coolness of the lobby into the brilliant sunshine outside was like stepping into a warm, humid shower room. Frank paused for a second to catch his breath, but Callie plowed straight ahead, right past the doorman.

7

After she stepped from under the hotel portico, Callie turned back to the Hardys to tell them to hurry up. Just at that moment Frank saw a tall, pale man in black jeans, a tight black T-shirt, and sunglasses running behind Callie on the sidewalk. He was aimed right for her—his arm straight out.

He didn't bump into her. He ran up to her and shoved. Callie tottered for an instant before falling to her knees. The assailant swooped down and reached for her, but not to help her. He helped himself instead.

Callie's purse was in his hands as he took off.

Chapter

2

FOR A BRIEF SECOND everyone froze. It was like a scene from a bad dream. Callie was down on the ground, the doorman stood staring, and Frank and Joe were rooted in place. The only one moving was the man with Callie's purse—he was halfway down the block.

Joe broke out first and burst into motion, taking off after the purse snatcher. Frank hurtled forward next, joining the pursuit. Behind them, the doorman blew his whistle, trying to attract a police officer.

Frank grinned without humor as he heard the shrill blast and kept on running. In his experience, there was never a cop around when you needed one.

He broke stride as he reached Callie, who had

gotten to her hands and knees. His girlfriend waved him on. "Forget about me—get that creep."

Frank kept on pounding along the pavement, trying to catch up with Joe, who was far ahead now. The man in black, however, was outdistancing them both. He whipped around the first corner, and by the time Joe reached it, the short block to his right was empty.

Joe didn't slow down, however. He pushed down that street to the next corner, where a street cut across the one he was on. Glancing right then left, Frank caught just a fleeting impression of a figure in black tearing around the far corner.

"This way," Joe gasped, pointing the way for his brother, who had caught up to him.

Rounding the next corner, they faced a large boulevard, with a huge open traffic circle beyond. The purse snatcher in black was weaving in and out of the midafternoon crowd. No one said anything to him. He only got a couple of annoyed glances—that was all. The guy moved too quickly for people to focus on him.

Frank realized that if he yelled the traditional "Stop that man!" people would hesitate a second and the guy would get past. No, they had to continue to chase him—and get him, too.

There was no place for the thief to hide. Frank and his brother could see around them for about four square blocks.

"How does this guy think he can lose us here?" Joe said.

"Maybe he doesn't know the neighborhood either," Frank panted as he kept up the pace.

The man in black didn't slow down. He darted through unseen gaps in the crowd like a running back on the way to the end zone. Apparently, he did know the area. He zigzagged through the traffic passing around the traffic circle, extending his lead over the Hardys. As they got closer, Frank and Joe saw their quarry run straight for a large concrete structure that looked like a gigantic funnel leading deep into the ground.

Joe skidded to a halt and turned to a young man walking by. "What's that?" he asked, pointing.

"Metro station," the passerby answered.

Frank dashed up at that moment. "The Washington subway—remember?"

Ahead of them, the purse snatcher was already beginning a broken-field run down the escalator to the train station and platform.

Joe leaped into the street, paying no attention to the taxi hurtling toward him. The brakes screeched as the cab swerved to another lane. Leaning out the window, the cab driver shouted something in a foreign language.

Frank took a deep breath and plunged into the traffic, too. It was like playing "chicken"—without a car. He had to dodge around and sidestep a couple of times.

At last they were across the street and on the escalator. The thief was already at the bottom. Frank and Joe got lots of dirty looks as they jostled their way down to the station lobby.

"There he is—running through a turnstile," Frank said, pointing.

Joe jumped the last few yards of the escalator and landed ready to run full tilt for the turnstiles. There he stopped dead, fumbling in his pockets. "How much is the fare?"

"Hey, kid, you have to go back and get a fare card." One of the regular subway riders pointed over his shoulder to a bank of what looked like vending machines. People were stepping up to them, slipping in coins and bills, and coming away with little computerized cards. Then they slipped the cards through a groove in the turnstile machines to enter the subway system.

Joe yanked out a handful of change and headed for the machines, but Frank grabbed his arm to stop him. The guy they'd been chasing was heading down another escalator. Below, they could hear a train arriving. "Too late, Joe," Frank said. "We've lost him."

Frank thought the trip back to the hotel seemed a lot longer than the journey out. Maybe that was because he and Joe had run one way, but were dragging their feet coming back.

Callie was standing in front of the hotel, where she was talking to a young police officer. He nodded very seriously as he took down her statement in his notebook. From the look on her face, he hadn't given her very much hope. "Did you catch the guy?" she asked eagerly as Frank walked up.

He shook his head. "He got away into the Metro station a few blocks away."

The police officer just shook his head. "I'm sorry to say this, but I think your chances of ever seeing that bag—and its contents—are pretty slim."

Callie's shoulders sagged. Frank went over and put an arm around her. "Are you okay?"

"I've just got a couple of bruises, but, Frank, all my money for the trip was in that purse!" She shook her head. "I guess I'm lucky that I brought it in traveler's checks, but all of Madeleine's letters were in there, too. I was going to leave them in the hotel, but she called and insisted that I bring them."

"Speaking of calls, maybe you should get on the phone to the Berots," Frank suggested. "They're probably wondering where we are."

Callie called and arranged to visit the Berots after she spoke to the desk clerk about replacing her traveler's checks.

The Berot family had settled in an old-fashioned brick apartment house not far from the hotel. It was an easy walk—now that there were no interruptions. Callie found the name Henri Berot on the intercom, and after a few moments she and her friends were buzzed into the building.

They arrived on the fifth floor to find an apartment door open and a tall, slim man standing in the doorway. He had thin, sharp features—a hatchet face, Frank's father would have called it—and his graying hair receded at the temples, forming a dramatic widow's peak. "Mademoiselle Shaw?" he said, a brief smile passing across his face. "And these are your friends? I am Henri Berot. Please come in."

Mr. Berot's smile faded as Callie and the Hardys followed him inside. Joe noticed that he immediately double-locked the door. "I am sorry for your trouble," the diplomat said. "This is a very dangerous city." He frowned. "Such lawlessness. Snatching of purses would not be tolerated back home."

Frank's eyebrows rose. "Well, Mr. Berot, whole countries can't be judged by looking at one city—or one area. I wouldn't judge France by the fact that it has so many trained gangs of child pickpockets."

Mr. Berot stiffened, offended. "You are insulting, Mr. Hardy. Has your pocket been picked in France? Your friend was stolen from *here*. If you think your home is safer, perhaps you should go back there."

He went on for several moments, his voice rising in anger at the "offense" to his homeland.

"Some diplomat," Callie whispered.

"Nice work, Frank," Joe added in a low voice. "We haven't even made it into the living room and you start World War Three—with France."

They could hardly understand what Mr. Berot was saying, since as his tirade went on he spoke more and more French. Just as he reached the shouting stage, two women appeared from the living room. A blond, middle-aged woman in a plain black dress rubbed her hands together nervously, then took Callie's hands in hers. "I am Sylvie Berot," she said. "And this, of course, is Madeleine—"

Sailing out from behind Madame Berot came a slim girl in jeans and a black satin baseball jacket. She grabbed Callie by the hands, kissed her on both cheeks, then turned angrily to her father.

Joe squinted, surprised. Maddy in person was a lot less pretty than her picture. Her voice was also high and whiny as she began arguing with her dad. Joe couldn't understand what they were saying. Both Berots spoke very rapidly in French. He glanced at Callie, who had taken French in school.

"Maddy's saying something about being tired of staying cooped up in the apartment. She wants to go out with us," she whispered.

While Callie and the Hardys stood in embarrassment, listening to an obvious argument, Mr. Berot finally turned to Mrs. Berot. She shook her head helplessly. He shrugged and abruptly held out an arm to escort his wife from the room.

Madeleine watched them go, then turned with a bright smile. "We can go out!" she said. "Callie, you have not introduced your friends."

"Maddy"—Callie turned to Joe and Frank—"I'd like you to meet—"

"What is this *Maddy?*" The smile quickly disappeared from the girl's face. "My name is Madeleine."

Callie blinked in puzzlement. "But in your letters . . ." Her voice trailed off.

"Hey, Madeleine," Joe tried to fill in. "We're sorry if—"

The French girl cut him off. "Not Mad-duh-linn," she said, mimicking Joe's pronunciation, making him feel like a real idiot. "It is a beautiful French name." She said it for him. "Madh-lenn."

"Okay, Modd . . . uh, Mah-deh-lenn." Frank watched the color glow in Joe's face as he stumbled over the name. Usually Joe picked up foreign words easily. Frank knew it was the unfriendly audience that made him hesitate now. It didn't help him to like Madeleine any better.

Madeleine rolled her eyes. "Maybe it's better that you call me Maddy," she said.

"Great family," Joe muttered to Frank as they headed for the elevator.

Frank nodded. "Very friendly."

"So," Callie said as they got into the elevator. "Where would you like to go, Maddy?"

Madeleine immediately took Callie's arm. "Shopping," she said with another dazzling smile.

Callie glanced over at Frank. "That might not be much fun for the boys. I thought maybe we could grab a snack and talk—"

"We can do that, too," Madeleine said. "But first, we shop."

They headed down Connecticut Avenue, popping in and out of the expensive boutiques that lined the street. Frank and Joe sighed and rolled their eyes as Callie and Madeleine flitted from skirts to shorts, from blouses to silk scarves.

Maddy was like a little kid, grabbing Callie's arm to show her a special item, hugging her. That brilliant smile kept lighting up her face.

Callie smiled back, but Frank thought she looked a little embarrassed as Maddy got louder and more excited. It was almost as if she'd never seen really good clothes before. How could that be when she came from Paris, the world capital of fashion?

Frank and Joe finally stopped going into the stores when the girls entered. They just watched through the window as Maddy moved through shops like a whirlwind, throwing an arm around

17

Callie to point out a special bargain or a beautiful outfit.

They stopped by the door to check a display of scarves, Maddy giggling and hugging Callie again.

As the girls came out, Frank asked, "More stores? Or have you had enough yet?"

"I've think I've had enough," Callie said. "Everything we've seen here I couldn't afford. How about you, Maddy?"

"Oh, I don't know—" Madeleine suddenly broke off. "What have you got there?"

The French girl pointed to the pocket of Callie's jacket, where a tiny piece of brightly colored fabric stuck out. Maddy tugged on it, pulling out a silk scarf—just like the ones the girls had admired inside the store.

"Callie, I never guessed. You are a clever one!" Madeleine burst out, handing the scarf back.

"Not so clever," a cold voice came from behind them.

The kids turned to see a salesclerk standing in the doorway. Her blond hair was wrapped in a bun, and her icy gray eyes were staring hard at Callie.

She pointed at the scarf in Callie's hands. "Most shoplifters don't flaunt stolen goods right in front of the store they took them from."

Chapter

3

CALLIE'S FACE went from bright red to dead white. "W-what are you talking about?" she asked, staring at the blond woman in the doorway.

"I'm talking about that scarf you just stole." The saleswoman's face was grim as she gestured to the door. "Now come back inside and we'll see what other 'bargains' you and your friend picked up."

The woman's glare included the Hardys. "You guys, too. They may have passed something on to you."

The four teens stood in a huddle by a rear counter, getting sidelong glances from customers as the manager of the store demanded IDs from them. Callie appeared to be numb as the manager

19

turned to her. "I—I don't have any," she stammered. "I just got into town, and my purse was stolen—"

The manager cut her off with a toss of her red curls. At any other time, Joe might have considered her pretty. He didn't right then, though—not with that superior sneer on her face. "Look, don't try some stupid sob story on me—I've heard them all. Now, how about some ID?"

Callie shrugged helplessly. "It's all been stolen. My friends will tell you what happened, and the police—"

"Oh, don't worry, honey, the police are coming, all right." The manager looked up as the saleswoman rejoined them. "You called the cops?" she asked.

The saleswoman nodded. "They're on their way."

"Police?" Callie repeated, still in a daze from the turn of events.

"That's what you usually do when you catch a thief," the salesclerk said.

"Take this one into the dressing room." The manager pointed to Callie. "I want her searched—thoroughly." The young woman moved to the Hardys. "You guys turn out your pockets on the counter, here."

Robotlike, Callie began to reach into her pockets, as well.

"Not you," the manager snapped. "I told you

already—you're going in the back for a full search.''

Callie recoiled from the angry face glaring at her. "This has never—I mean, I've never—'' she began haltingly, but the other woman cut her off.

'' 'Done this before in my life?' '' The red-haired woman's voice mimicked Callie's. "Well, maybe you should have thought of that before you tried to take something that didn't belong to you.''

The saleswoman took Callie's arm. She was shaking as she was led off a couple of steps. She glanced back at Frank, her tear-filled eyes begging him to do something to help.

"Let's just cut this nonsense right now.'' Frank's voice was angry as he stepped forward to protect his girlfriend. "You'll see from our ID that I'm Frank Hardy and this is my brother Joe.''

"Hardy, huh?'' The manager was definitely not impressed. "As far as I know, we don't have a Senator Hardy. So who are you? Some congressman's kids? Or maybe your dad is a big mucka-muck at the State Department?'' She seemed rather amused by Frank's outburst. "We get all kinds here.''

Frank sighed. This wasn't Bayport, where people knew the Hardys and their reputation. And from the look of things, claiming a famous detective for a father wasn't going to cut much ice with this woman.

Like it or not, Frank—and Callie—would have to put up with a lot of flak until the Washington police checked with Chief Collig back in Bayport. Frank tried to dig up the name of any of his dad's friends on the D.C. force. No luck.

"Let's just get on with it," the woman said. Callie was marched to the back.

Frank's mind had already leaped ahead to the next problem—the police. Callie had been caught with a stolen scarf in her pocket. That would be hard to explain—even if he got a sympathetic ear from one of his father's friends. He knew Callie hadn't shoplifted!

He said so to the manager, but she only shrugged.

"Kids think the world owes them everything— always coming in here trying to lift stuff. Rich kids, college kids, even tourists," the woman growled, checking out the Hardys' Bayport High IDs.

The manager whirled on Madeleine. "Don't you grin, girlie. You're the next one going back to be searched."

That got her a murderous glare from the French girl.

The saleswoman returned. "This one is clean— all she had was the scarf." Callie walked behind the woman, her clothes rumpled and her face a picture of humiliation. Tears began to spill out of her eyes. "I don't know how that scarf got in my jacket, but I didn't put it there," she insisted.

Neither the saleswoman nor the store manager listened to her. "This one goes next," the manager said, pointing to Madeleine.

The French girl looked ready to deck the two women. "No one touches me," she snarled.

Glancing out the store window, the manager shrugged. "I see the cops are here. They can take care of searching her at the station."

Two police officers entered. "These the kids?" they asked the manager, pointing to the Hardys and the girls.

The woman nodded. "Hold on a moment," she said, stepping into the back of the store. A moment later she reappeared, holding a videocassette. "Another piece of evidence. We tape everything that goes on in the store. You'll probably have a lovely shot of Blondie over there stealing the scarf." Without another glance at the kids, she turned to a customer.

The ride to the local police station was quiet and cramped. All four kids were squashed into the back of the police squad car. Callie cried quietly the entire way. Frank held her hand, his face stiff. When he found out who was responsible for getting Callie in trouble, he'd make the person pay—and pay hard.

Madeleine squirmed in her seat, then grabbed Callie's free hand. "Don't worry," she said. "Everything will turn out okay. I'll take care of it."

Callie stared at her for a second. "How?" she finally asked.

They arrived at the station and were unceremoniously led into a waiting room. After they'd spent almost an hour sitting on a wooden bench, a man in shirtsleeves and a shoulder holster came in.

"I'm Detective Cook," he said. "Follow me." They filed silently along to what looked like an interrogation room. This one, however, had a television set and a VCR. The policeman gestured to a group of wooden chairs spread out in front of the set. "We thought you might like to see this," he said, punching a button.

On the TV screen, the image of the boutique appeared. The angle of the shot was weird—it seemed to come from the ceiling. Of course, Frank realized, that's where the security cameras must be hidden.

In spite of the strange point of view, the picture was clear. There were Frank and Joe standing outside the window, pacing up and down as if they were bored out of their minds. And there, by the doorway, were Callie and Madeleine, looking at the scarves.

Maddy turned to Callie with a big grin, hugging

her. At the same time the French girl slipped the gaily colored silk scarf into Callie's pocket.

Callie jumped in her seat as if it were electrified. She turned to Madeleine, her eyes still red with tears. *"You* did this to me?" she finally managed to say.

"Oh, Callie," Madeleine said, grabbing her hands, "I am so, so sorry. It was only supposed to be a little *plaisanterie,* a joke. Then that fool of a salesgirl came out and made so much trouble. I . . . didn't know what to say."

She turned to the detective, giving him her 150-watt smile. "These are my American friends, you see," she said, her French accent becoming a bit more pronounced. "I met them today for the first time. What I did with the scarf, that was only a joke."

Maddy patted Callie's shoulder. "Poor Callie, here, she had her purse stolen. So I thought to make her laugh, you see? I would have paid for the scarf, but the woman wouldn't listen, and the manager was insulting to me. I will pay now, and then everything will be okay, yes?" Joe thought that Maddy looked downright cute as she looked up at Detective Cook.

The frowning police officer didn't seem to think so, however. He was shaking his head. "I'm afraid it isn't as easy as that," he said. "The manager of the store has sworn out a complaint for theft. You admit you took the scarf without paying for it. Under the law—"

Madeleine's face turned ugly as she glared at the man. "What do I care about the American law?" she burst out. "I am a French citizen."

"That doesn't—" Detective Cook started, but Maddy cut him off again.

With a contemptuous toss of her head, she said, "*And* I have diplomatic immunity."

Chapter

4

JOE HARDY FELT as if he were watching a very fast tennis game. His eyes moved back and forth from Maddy to Callie, to Frank, who looked as if he were going to burst a blood vessel when he heard Maddy was responsible for the whole mess. His eyes darted back to Maddy when she claimed diplomatic immunity.

She dug through her bag and came up with a small blue booklet, which she pressed into Detective Cook's hand.

He paged through it, sighed, and went to the door. "Our shoplifter has a French diplomatic passport. Better call Lieutenant Grant."

They had a much shorter wait for this investigator than for the station house detective. I guess

27

international incidents get a lot faster service from the D.C. police, Joe thought.

Lieutenant Grant turned out to be a tall black man, dressed in a well-cut gray silk suit. Comparing his expensive clothes to the rumpled, cheap ones of Cook, Joe decided the Washington police *did* make a big deal out of possible international incidents.

The lieutenant held the gaily colored scarf that had turned up in Callie's pocket. Grant spoke for a minute with Detective Cook. As they conferred in whispers, the lieutenant kept shooting glances over at Madeleine—the way a person would check out a strange animal that could be dangerous.

The detective ran the videotape again while Grant watched. The lieutenant then rubbed his face with one hand and began speaking. "I've gone over the reports on this case and gotten the latest wrinkles from Detective Cook here." He nodded at the other man. "I'd like to get statements from all of you—"

A "harrumph" from the doorway interrupted Lieutenant Grant's flow. Everyone turned to see a short man standing just inside the door. His blue suit, elegantly cut, just called attention to his skinny frame and knobby knees. With his white shirt and red bow tie, Joe thought he looked like a cross between Jiminy Cricket and Uncle Sam.

28

The man cleared his throat again. "Ambrose Wilmer—State Department," he announced.

"Nice to see you again, Mr. Wilmer." From the tone of Lieutenant Grant's voice, Frank figured that was an out-and-out lie. "Been a long time."

"Approximately three weeks," Wilmer corrected him prissily. "You failed to inform me of this new case, Lieutenant. Luckily, I happened to be in contact with your office just now. I've taken the liberty of informing the young lady's father already. He assured me that he would be arriving momentarily."

Henri Berot appeared behind the State Department man just then. The look on his face reminded Frank of Joe's earlier joke—how Mr. Berot was ready to start World War Three. Right then, if Mr. Berot would have had anything to say about it, the French army would be on the march.

He spared one searing glance for his daughter, then turned on Lieutenant Grant. "This—this Wilmer person called me at my home to tell me that the police are holding my daughter," he said angrily. "He said something ridiculous about her stealing a scarf."

"Now, now, Mr. Berot." Wilmer's voice tried to sound soothing but came across more like a set of fingernails on a blackboard. "I'm sure the report is exaggerated."

"I'm afraid not, Mr. Wilmer," Lieutenant Grant said. He stepped over to the VCR and rewound the tape. As it started playing again, he said to Madeleine, "I guess you're getting pretty tired of seeing this."

She only shrugged. "Good practice in case I decide to become a movie star."

Fuming, Mr. Berot almost shouted the words, "Start it!"

He sat in absolute silence as the scene of Madeleine's slipping the scarf into Callie's pocket played. When Lieutenant Grant moved to stop the tape, he suddenly spoke up. "Bring it back— all the way back to when they entered the store."

Lieutenant Grant paused in midmotion to stare at Mr. Berot.

"I want to see *everything* that happened in that store," Berot said.

Grant's eyebrows rose. "You think we're hiding something here?"

"I know my daughter would not do something like this—unless she had been led into it." Berot glanced at the Hardys and Callie. "In the few weeks I've been here, I've found America to be a very dangerous country. People—especially young people—have no respect for the law."

Lieutenant Grant started the VCR again. They watched the girls' entire visit to the boutique— right up to the unfortunate ending.

"It appears that Miss Shaw did nothing suspicious,'' Lieutenant Grant said. ''In fact, she seemed somewhat embarrassed even before the shoplifting incident.''

Mr. Berot shook his head. ''This videotape proves nothing. I think it is these wild American kids—*they* are responsible. Maybe they dared my Madeleine to steal something before they went in. Did you think of that?''

''In any event, Ms. Berot is indeed protected by diplomatic immunity,'' Mr. Wilmer said. The State Department man gave them all a rabbity smile. ''We would prefer to end this incident with as little publicity as possible.''

Berot nodded abruptly, pulling out a wallet. He quickly counted some bills onto the table beside the VCR. ''This should cover the price of the scarf.''

He snatched up the silk scarf that had started all the trouble and thrust it into Madeleine's hands.

Maddy, however, lagged behind her father. She pressed the scarf into Callie's hands. ''Callie, you keep this. I'm very sorry for what happened. At least you aren't in trouble anymore. I'll call you tomorrow at your hotel. Maybe I can find some way to make this up to you.'' She ran from the interrogation room before Callie could say anything. Wilmer had already set off after Mr. Berot.

''Wilmer is usually more interested in soothing

a diplomat's ruffled feathers than dealing with American civilians," Lieutenant Grant said to Frank, Joe, and Callie. "He usually leaves that menial stuff to me."

The lieutenant gave them all a long look. "Officially, you are free to go. Unofficially, I have some advice for you." He raised his hand when he saw Callie jump from her seat and head for the door. "It's not a long lecture—just a quick line. When Madeleine Berot calls you tomorrow, don't answer the phone." Grant shook his head. "Trust an old cop's instincts—that kid is trouble."

A few minutes later Callie, Joe, and Frank were out of the police station and on the street. Callie made her exit on wobbly legs. "I feel like a dish towel that's been wrung out—about five times."

"It's a long walk back to the hotel," Frank said.

Joe nodded. "Yeah—I wish Lieutenant Grant had given us a lift back instead of his advice."

Callie shook her head. "No way. I've had enough cops today."

Joe dug a guide to Washington out of his back pocket. "There's a Metro station nearby. Feel up to a short ride, Callie?"

Callie glanced at her watch. "It's not rush hour yet. So far, this has been the worst day of my life."

They took the escalator down to the station

lobby, to find a rank of fare card vending machines. "I'll pay for each of us," Joe offered.

He slipped a dollar into the machine, hit a button, and out popped a fare card, which he handed to Callie. Another dollar went in, and out came another card. Joe handed it to Frank. But when he tried to slip his next bill in, the machine spat it out.

"Look at this thing," Joe said, holding it up. "This has to be the world's worst-looking dollar bill. It must have gone through a washing machine." The dollar was limp and worn, looking almost chewed on.

Digging another bill out of his jeans, Joe slipped it in, got his card, and headed for the turnstiles.

As they rode the escalator down to the platform, lights set into the concrete began to flash. "Hey, we're in luck," Frank said. "There's a train on the way."

They began to run down the escalator. The train still hadn't reached the station when they reached the platform.

Callie moved to the edge of the platform, peering down the tunnel to watch for moving lights.

Joe saw a thin man in sunglasses, tight black jeans, and a skimpy, European-cut shirt walk up behind her. As he came up to Callie, he didn't step around her. Instead, he purposely bumped into her, sending her staggering toward the edge of the platform.

"Callie!" Frank yelled, whipping around to grab his girlfriend's arm before she fell onto the tracks.

The thin guy sprinted away, cutting in and out of the crowd waiting on the platform.

"*This* one isn't getting away," Joe muttered to himself grimly as he took off after the guy along the platform.

His quarry raced ahead, but Joe was the Bayport football team's best broken-field runner. He closed in quickly.

The guy darted to the edge of the platform, trying to wriggle through the heart of the crowd to lose Joe.

It didn't work. In another minute Joe stretched out an arm and caught him by the shoulder.

"Don't be shy, buddy," Joe said. "Turn around. We have to go back and you can apologize to our friend. Then maybe you might explain why you almost knocked her onto the tracks."

The man did turn around, and Joe gawked. He knew him! Same sunglasses, same dark hair, and a black T-shirt showed at the neck of his European-cut shirt. This was the same person who'd snatched Callie's purse! The man's hand came out of his pocket, clenched in a fist. Joe moved, ready to block a blow, but this guy wasn't throwing a punch. His hand opened about a foot from Joe's face, releasing a cloud of reddish powder.

Joe blinked in surprise—until the powder hit

his face. He began coughing and sneezing as the orangy red particles got into his nose and throat. His eyes hurt the worst. They burned as if someone had thrown acid in them.

Suddenly blinded, Joe recoiled. His antagonist gave him a vicious shove, and Joe staggered backward, his arms flailing in large windmill patterns. His right foot stepped back and found only air under it.

He was going over the edge of the platform— just as the train was coming in!

Chapter

5

As HE FELL OFF the platform, Joe heard and felt a rumbling sound. The train was coming in! He landed hard in the track area and lay stunned for a moment, the air knocked out of him.

He had no time to stay there and catch his breath. He forced his tearing eyes open and got a blurry view of the track bed in front of him. All he could see was a pair of oncoming headlights. The train was nearly on top of him, with no time or space to brake. If Joe tried leaping for the edge of the platform, the train would probably hit him in midair. There was no way he could outrun it.

His thoughts fast-forwarded. If he couldn't outrun or go over the onrushing train, there was only one way to avoid being squashed like a bug. That was to go under it.

Joe lay in the center of the track bed, pressing his body flat between the rails. He was just in time. The carriages swooped over him with a swoosh of cold air. Joe pressed his face to the track bed. His entire body shook as the train screeched to a stop. A chill ran along his spine—partly from the breeze made by the stopping cars, but mostly from terror.

Wiggling his way to the closest opening between cars, Joe finally managed to scramble back onto the platform.

Callie and Frank came rushing up. "Joe! Joe! Are you okay?" Callie shouted.

"Just great," Joe said, rubbing a bruised shoulder. "The guy who almost nailed you had some nastiness left over. So he gave it to me—right down to the rails. Believe it or not, he blinded me with a handful of cayenne pepper." Joe blinked his still-bleary eyes. "Where did he go?"

"He disappeared into the crowd when you fell." Frank shook his head. "I was with Callie—and too far away."

"I'm sorry, Joe," Callie said. The train began to pull out of the station.

Joe laughed as he watched it disappear into the nearest tunnel. They had missed their train after all that. "I suggest a vote," he said. "Those in favor of a cab back to the hotel raise their hands."

His hand and Callie's immediately shot into the

air. Frank stared after the train for a second, thinking. Then in a distracted way he raised his hand as well.

They spent a gloomy evening in Callie's room, eating a room-service meal. Callie hardly touched her food. She just sat on the couch, looking blue. Frank sat beside her and held her hand. "You okay?"

Callie shrugged. "You know, I've been looking forward to this trip for weeks. It was all going to be perfect, like a dream, meeting a friend I'd never seen before." She shook her head. "Instead it's been a nightmare. Three times today, something awful has happened—or nearly happened—to me."

Joe laughed. "So what do you think, Callie? Is this a plot against you?" He pretended to pull out a notebook. "Tell us, Miss Shaw, do you have any enemies in the Washington area?" Then he turned to Frank. "Maybe we should round up the usual suspects."

"That's not funny, Joe," Frank said.

Callie took her hand out of his. "I got both you guys in trouble, and Joe nearly got killed." She sighed. "And let's face it, Madeleine Berot hasn't turned out to be the perfect friend."

"She ought to be arrested for false advertising, sending you a picture that made her look like a knockout," Joe complained. "But she'd probably get out of it by claiming diplomatic immunity."

Callie refused to be cheered up by Joe's joking around. "Guys, I'm thinking about cutting this vacation short. Maybe we can get a flight home tomorrow."

"Bayport's beginning to look better and better," Joe admitted. Before he could say anything more, the phone rang.

Callie picked up the receiver. "Yes?" she said, then her face froze. "Oh, hello, Maddy. No, I wasn't asleep. I was sitting here with the guys."

She beckoned the Hardys closer, holding up the phone so they could hear Madeleine's voice.

"My father was *furious* over what happened," Maddy said. "I thought he was going to—what do you call it—ground me. I'll probably have to stay around the house tomorrow and get him calmed down. But what are you doing tomorrow night?"

Callie stared at the receiver, speechless.

Maddy's voice rushed on. "I know you should be angry at me for that stupid joke. But I didn't mean for it to turn out the way it did. I was going to tell you to watch your pockets, then go back and pay for the scarf. Instead, that crazy woman came out and started making accusations."

"You still might have explained," Callie said stiffly.

"I should have," Maddy agreed, her voice contrite. "Things just moved so quickly—and those women were all ready to believe the worst about us. It is all my fault, and I'm very, very sorry."

The French girl's voice brightened. "Anyway, I want to make up for all of it. There's a new club that's opened not far from your hotel—the Quarter. It's supposed to be really hot. I hear that all the kids from diplomatic families hang out there."

Now Madeleine's voice grew pleading. "Would you, Joe, and Frank like to go there tomorrow night? It will be my treat."

Callie looked as if Maddy had just invited her out for a mud fight. "I don't know," she began hesitantly.

Apparently, Frank did. He tapped Callie's shoulder to get her attention, vigorously nodding his head up and down.

Joe was surprised by his brother's enthusiasm. Back at the police station, Joe had seen Frank's face when he realized that Maddy was responsible for Callie's trouble. Joe thought Frank had been ready to unscrew Maddy's head from her neck—without tools. Now he wanted to make a date for all of them to go out with her.

Joe was about to make a joke about it until he caught the serious expression on his brother's face. Frank seemed to have more than dancing on his mind. Unless Joe was badly mistaken, his brother had a case to think about.

"Okay," Callie said, scribbling down the address of the club. "The Quarter, at eight-thirty. See you then."

Callie hung up the phone, staring at Frank. "Lieutenant Grant said to stay away from Maddy—how come you want to go dancing with her?"

"Call it a hunch," Frank said.

Joe was startled and stared at his brother. He was the one with hunches in this investigating team.

"Somebody seems to be going out of his—or her—way to make our visit to Washington as unpleasant as possible," Frank said. "Somehow we may have wandered into someone's way. And that someone may be up to something big."

Now Callie was staring at Frank, too. "I don't think I'm ready to buy a conspiracy theory to ruin our vacation," she objected.

"Frank may not be as crazy as you think," Joe suddenly said. "I didn't mention it before, but I think the guy who tried to push you on the tracks was the same one who stole your purse."

Frank turned to him, eyes blazing. "Are you sure?"

Joe shrugged. "If I was, I wouldn't have said, 'I think.' He had the same shades on, and under his shirt was a black T-shirt."

"So we have a firm *maybe*." Frank looked over at Callie. "But you may have had a good idea before. You know, about heading back to Bayport, while we—"

"While you guys look into things? No way, François," Callie said emphatically. "Either we all stay and check this out, or we all go."

Frank and Joe exchanged a quick glance and a shrug. They knew they'd get nowhere when Callie used that tone of voice.

Joe yawned and stretched. "It's been a long day. I'm going to hit the sack." He headed for the door, then stopped. "I'll expect to see you soon—*after* you've said good night." He headed for his room, grinning because he'd been able to make both Frank and Callie blush.

The next morning at breakfast nobody mentioned the conspiracy theory. Frank, Joe, and Callie decided to act like typical tourists and explore the two-mile long Washington Mall, with all its famous museums.

They stopped moving back and forth on the gravel paths long enough to gaze at the red sandstone walls of the Smithsonian Castle. "It's so weird. It looks like somebody dropped a huge castle right in the middle of Washington," Callie said. "What do they keep in it, the National Armor Collection?"

"It used to be a museum, but now it's full of

offices and things like that," Frank said, consulting his guidebook. "The building next door has all sorts of great stuff, though."

"Great stuff" was just what they found next door in the Arts and Industries Building. The sprightly, bright-colored brick building contained everything from Indian totem poles to an old-fashioned train locomotive.

"That was pretty cool," Joe said as they walked back out into the sunshine forty-five minutes later.

"There's a modern art museum nearby," Callie said. "Want to check it out?"

Joe stared at the round bulk of the Hirshhorn Museum. "Looks like a giant concrete pillbox," he said.

"It's more like a doughnut," Frank said, his nose back in the guidebook.

They explored three floors of modern art, and enjoyed a great view of the Mall from the museum's balcony room.

"Going to become a painter now, Joe?" Callie teased as they went back.

"Only if Dad catches up with me and makes me do the garage," Joe said.

"An awful fate." Frank laughed. "Tell you what—you choose the next museum."

"I think we've seen enough art for a while. How about animals?"

They trudged across the central grassy space

of the Mall to the Natural History Museum. "Nice effect," Frank said as they stepped through the entrance to find themselves confronted with a gigantic stuffed elephant.

"Your turn," Callie said to Frank after they toured that museum for an hour.

"I bet High-tech Hardy picks something with machines," Joe said.

"You read my mind," Frank told him with a grin. "How about the National Air and Space Museum?"

Back across the Mall again, they headed for a huge glass, marble, and steel building. The first airplane from 1903 and the first American space capsule to orbit the earth were inside. Not only that, there were hundreds of other fascinating pieces of flight and space technology.

They started into the museum cafeteria for a late lunch at two-thirty. "So what do you think?" Frank asked.

"I just wish we could take longer in each museum. We barely skimmed the surface of each of them," Callie complained.

Joe, however, didn't answer. He threw a puzzled glance over his shoulder.

"What's the problem, Joe?" Callie asked.

For an answer Joe threw an arm around Frank and Callie and turned them around. He headed for the escalators. "Don't all look at once, but there's a guy behind us."

"Dark suit, straw hat?" Frank said, pretending to kid with Callie so he could steal a peek.

"That's the one. Have you seen him before?"

Callie angled for a quick look, then shook her head. "I've never seen him before."

"Well, I have," Joe said grimly. "We've been zipping back and forth between these museums at random. This guy has popped up at the last three places we've visited."

"He likes our taste in museums?" Callie tried to sound light about it, but she didn't succeed.

Joe picked up the pace. "Let's face it, guys," he said. "We're being followed."

Chapter

6

"LET'S GET OUT of here." Frank kept up the cheerful act by smiling, but his voice came out tight and strained. He steered them quickly through a couple of exhibits at the museum, not wanting to warn their shadow that he'd been spotted.

"What do we do now?" Callie asked.

"If we were alone, I'd suggest leading the guy tailing us to a quiet corner where we could ask him what he's doing," Joe answered Callie. "But the problem is, we're not alone—"

"Now wait a minute," Callie burst out. "We've been on enough cases together that you should know I can carry my weight."

"Let's quit arguing and just lose this clown." Frank felt his temper rising because of the squabbling. They had a job to do now. Maybe later, when they had a better shot at their tail, they could confront him. But this wasn't the time.

"How do we lose him?" Callie asked.

"Just look out there." Joe nodded toward the mass of tourists on the Mall. "Frank and I have lost tails in smaller crowds than that."

Frank led the way out of the museum, using the huge plate-glass windows around them as mirrors to check on their tail.

The man following them was hardly a character who blended into the crowd. He was a short, heavyset man wearing a dark suit, no tie, dark glasses, and a straw hat. He had at least a day's growth of beard on his round face. He was vaguely foreign looking, but he didn't look like a tourist. He looked like a well-dressed slob.

Well, they'd find out how sloppy he was in a minute. Once out of the museum Frank led his brother and Callie into a gap in the crowd. A mob of people soon filed in behind them, cutting them off from Shorty, as Frank had nicknamed their pursuer. He was a good tail, but following the Hardys and Callie now would be like swimming against the current.

Frank grinned as the man fell behind them. "That was simple enough," he said.

"Not as simple as you think." Joe jerked his head over his left shoulder.

Frank checked and spotted another man keeping pace with them.

This follower was tall and thin, with long, greasy black hair. His skinny frame was only emphasized by the loud Hawaiian shirt he wore. Three of him could have fit inside its billows. This guy, too, wore sunglasses. He was too far away for Frank to make out his face clearly, but he did resemble the purse snatcher and the guy at the Metro. Of course, it might just be that he looked like the other guy—a young, greasy punk.

Frank could tell his brother was thinking the same thoughts. All Joe said was, "He picked us up as soon as we left the museum."

"Great," Frank muttered. "Now we've got to peel this guy off, too. It won't be as easy. He's got to be suspicious."

Frank led the way, following one of the gravel paths. "There's a Metro station about two and a half blocks away, near the National Archives," he said. "Maybe we can jog down there and pull the same trick the purse snatcher pulled on us."

It could have been a good plan, but it didn't work. They hadn't gotten even halfway across the Mall when Frank picked up yet another man cutting across the grass to move in ahead of them. Unlike Shorty and Mr. Hawaii, as he decided to call the guy in the loud shirt, this follower looked dangerous.

He was tall and stocky, built like a bull, with a

head smaller than it should have been. He wore a garish sport coat and tight pants, and both appeared to be foreign cut. He was also wearing sunglasses.

Using the regulation sunglasses, Frank made out a big, puffy nose like a potato, sagging cheeks, and an oversize, jutting chin. The guy's yellowish, unhealthy-looking face was covered with pockmarks.

Joe caught sight of the new player in this scary game of tag. "That guy could be on a poster for the War Against Zits," he joked.

"Looks like Old Ugly's been sent in to cut us off," Frank said, changing course.

They abruptly turned and headed back the way they had come. "There's another Metro station beyond the Air and Space Museum—a big one, with lots of trains going through."

They could just see the two guys they'd left behind circling around to cut them off. And just then Frank thought he saw someone else in sunglasses moving their way.

"What do we do now?" Callie wanted to know. "These guys obviously know that we've seen them. They're not going to let us ditch them."

It was a ridiculous situation, Frank thought. Here they were, in one of the most heavily visited areas of the nation's capital, surrounded by tourists, being tailed by three or four men. The afternoon sun shone brightly down on the open green space, reflecting off the limestone, marble, glass, and steel fronts of the distinguished museums and offices that lined the Mall. It was crazy that this should be happening there in bright daylight.

Frank felt as if he were wearing a target on his head. He had been afraid that their followers would catch up to them in an isolated spot. Now, from the way these guys were moving in and cutting off every escape route, they could be planning to pull something right in the middle of the crowd.

"Frank," Joe said, "we've got to find a way out of here—*fast!*"

"Unless you can call down a helicopter or an air strike, I don't think we're getting out of here," Callie said.

"We'll have to settle for something a little more down-to-earth," Frank answered. He grabbed Callie's hand and sprinted forward, with Joe following close behind, as if heading for the open space between the two men who blocked the way back to the Air and Space Museum. The two thugs moved together, filling in the hole.

Frank then abruptly changed course, and they all climbed on board one of the Tourmobile buses that constantly circled the Mall. Frank paid all three fares to the driver. Just as the bus began pulling away, Old Ugly managed to get on. His partners, however, were too far away to catch up.

"Nice going, Frank. At least you cut down the

odds," Joe whispered with a glance at the large plug-ugly who stood by the front door.

"For the moment," Callie said, looking out the window. Far behind them, two of their shadows were running along behind the bus.

The kids sat quietly until the bus reached its next stop. At the last possible moment they burst out. Old Ugly was caught by surprise as they left the bus, but he managed to pry the doors open and get off, too.

Callie and the Hardys had a big lead and ran hard, passing the huge reflecting pool, before they stumbled up a set of marble stairs. Above them was a statue of General Grant sitting on his horse and looking grim. They ran past him, then past a statuary group of charging calvary troopers. That's just what we need right now, Frank thought—the cavalry to come charging to the rescue.

The bronze soldiers didn't leap into action, so Frank kept moving, keeping pace with Joe and Callie as they headed for Capitol Hill.

Ahead of them now rose the gleaming white marble of the Capitol Building, with its huge, soaring dome. From not far behind them, Frank could hear the pounding of footsteps up the marble steps of the Grant Monument. Taking a second to glance back, he saw that Old Ugly was pretty close on their tail. The pockmarked man moved fast for a man of his weight.

Frank's blood froze as he watched their tail reach under his loud sport coat, but the man suddenly stiffened, and his hand came away empty. Turning toward the Capitol, Frank saw an armed police officer stroll toward them. "Take it easy, kids," the guard told them. "The Capitol's been here almost two hundred years. It's not going to disappear before you get there."

Frank glanced nervously at Joe. Should he tell the police officer they were being followed? Would he believe it? Even Frank didn't know what was going on. "Okay, sir," he said, slowing down his pace.

Callie, who'd been about to spill everything, shut her mouth with an audible snap. Shrugging her shoulders, she walked quietly toward the entrance.

That lasted for about ten seconds. "Why didn't we get that cop to help us?" she whispered furiously to Frank.

"He wouldn't have believed me," Frank told her. "Besides, I've got a better plan."

They joined a line of tourists in the entrance-way, walking through a small metal archway. As one of the people ahead of them stepped through, a loud buzzer went off. The man stepped back and started going through his pockets, removing coins and keys.

"A metal detector!" Joe said, grinning as he began to understand.

52

He glanced behind them. Old Ugly, seeing the metal detector, hung back at the entryway, his hand almost protectively going under his left arm.

"If he's carrying a gun—and it looks like he is—he can't come through the detector." Joe grinned. "Nice move, Frank."

"So, we could go straight through the Rotunda, out the other side, and lose him," Callie said.

"Or . . ." Frank's voice trailed off.

"Or?" Callie prompted.

"We could let them send a guy in after us—unarmed—and face him down in here," Joe said. "That's what you were thinking, right?"

Frank nodded, checking out the large round room, crowded with tourists. "I wonder, though, if Congress will lend us a committee room for a real, in-depth interview."

"We'll just have to see," Joe said, his eyes lighting up at the promise of action.

Back at the doorway, the rest of the pursuers had joined up with Old Ugly. They seemed to be arguing with him. Through a trick of acoustics, Frank caught two words from the man. *"Le coup."* Then, using the others to shield him, he slipped something to one of his accomplices and headed through the metal detector.

Callie, Frank, and Joe joined the end of a tour group that was just leaving, Old Ugly grimly trailing them. They saw officers' and committee rooms, then went underground to the subway system that ran between lawmakers' offices and the Capitol.

As they entered the underground area, the three kids held back as the main group boarded a train. Frank and Joe moved to confront Old Ugly.

The big thug paid no attention to them. Reaching into his coat, he whipped out what seemed to be a thin piece of paper. What was he going to do? Frank wondered. Give them a paper cut?

Frank suddenly realized that the white object in the man's hand wasn't paper—it was a five-inch knife blade. "Watch out!" he yelled.

Old Ugly was already on the move, knife extended—aiming straight for Callie Shaw.

Chapter

7

FRANK LEAPED FORWARD as the blade in the huge thug's hand went straight for Callie's throat. Joe was there first, though, knocking the knife off-course. It flashed inches from her face as she scrambled back.

Even as he struggled with Joe for the knife, Old Ugly swung out with his free hand. Frank winced as the thug's openhanded blow sent Joe flying into the wall, stunned.

That left only Frank between the killer and Callie. He stood his ground, raising his hands in an almost pleading gesture. "Now wait a minute, big fella. Can't we talk about this?"

The ugly face looming over him twisted into a nasty smile. Old Ugly shook his head no.

Frank shrugged. "Okay, then." His foot lashed

out to catch Old Ugly in the shin. The big guy leaped back one step with a roar. He instantly limped forward, though, brandishing his knife. Frank began to wonder if the confrontation in the temporarily empty area had been such a bright idea.

As soon as the thought came, the area was no longer empty. A man in a suit—maybe a senator, maybe a legislative aide—walked up, reading some papers. When he saw the guy with the knife, he threw up his hands, the papers went flying, and he ran back along the corridor, screaming. Frank just hoped help would come before he was sliced and diced.

Old Ugly was taking him a lot more seriously now, advancing slowly in a knife fighter's crouch. The blade was out, flicking slowly back and forth. Unarmed and unable to get past the knife, all Frank could do was retreat.

The area was still completely empty. Anyone who did come in ran screaming when they saw the knife-wielding Old Ugly. Frank hoped Callie had the sense to get out of there. He didn't dare turn around to look for her—not with that strange-looking white knife just inches from his heart.

Old Ugly feinted left, then right, then drove the knife straight at Frank's chest.

Frank's attention was riveted on the blade—he didn't see Joe launch off the wall in a wild leap.

The knife swung wildly as Joe plowed into Old Ugly, who struggled to stay upright. With a guy this big, they had to keep at him until he went down all the way.

Frank twisted the thug's knife arm fiercely, smashing it down on his knee. Old Ugly lost his grip, and the knife dropped to the tile floor.

As soon as the white blade hit the ground, it shattered.

"No wonder he got that thing through the metal detectors," Frank said. "It's made of ceramic!"

His momentary distraction nearly got him decked. Old Ugly had wrenched his arm free and was swinging at him. Frank ducked, and the big thug pulled away, moving fast despite his limp. Joe grabbed for him, but Old Ugly was free now, lumbering down the corridor. Passengers from a train that had just arrived hit the walls as he plowed through them.

Frank grabbed Joe's arm and led him in the opposite direction. Joe pulled against his lead. "Come on, Joe, you've got to know when to end a fight. We'll never catch him," Frank said.

Callie came running back to them. "Let's join up with that tour," she said, pointing. "Then we can get out of here," she said.

Frank shrugged. "Sounds good to me."

They blended in with the tourist group and headed back for the Rotunda. The whole Hill was swarming with Capitol police—and there was no sign of Old Ugly or any of the other tails.

"I guess they got scared off," Callie said. "I don't know about you guys, but I think I've done enought sight-seeing for today."

"Yeah," Joe agreed. "I'm in the mood for a nice cab ride back to our hotel."

As they pulled up at the hotel entrance, Joe pulled out his wallet. He counted out the money for the fare and found that worn bill that wouldn't go into the fare card machine. For a second he grinned, almost tempted to use the Worst Dollar Bill in the World for the trip. But he was afraid the driver might run over his foot as he pulled away.

"I am ready to sleep till next Wednesday," Callie said as they rode up in the elevator.

"Well, you'll have to cram your rest into what's left of the afternoon," Frank said. "We're going to the Quarter tonight, remember?"

Callie stared at him. "You're kidding, right? We nearly got killed, and you still want to go out tonight?"

Joe's eyes narrowed as he looked at his brother. "Maybe that's how he expects to find out who's been trying to kill us."

The Quarter was in a new building on a small side street off Connecticut Avenue. It was pretty easy to find. The Hardys and Callie just had to look for a place with a lot of kids hanging around outside—and lots of expensive cars parked nearby. Joe stopped halfway down the block. "Check this one out, guys. A Porsche convertible."

"Right now, I want to check out Maddy," Frank said. "And her friends," he added hastily when he saw Callie's raised eyebrows.

Madeleine Berot was already in the club, dancing up a storm. Her partner was a tall, good-looking blond guy, dressed in a tapered raw linen shirt. The lights flickered and the music was loud, and Maddy's dancing was wild and abandoned.

"What do you think?" Frank shouted over the noise.

Joe shrugged. "Looks pretty good to me."

There was a break in the music, and Madeleine ran over to them. "You came! You came!" she shouted. "I'm so happy!"

Her blond friend strolled over with her. By the look on his face, he wasn't too glad to see the newcomers. "This is Ansel," Madeleine said, patting his shoulder. "His father works at the German embassy."

"What a surprise," Joe muttered.

"I met him and his friends here," Maddy went on. "They're all diplomats' kids."

"Dips and dip-ettes," Frank whispered to Callie, staring at the elaborately dressed guys and girls Madeleine was pointing toward.

"What is the story with you?" Ansel asked. "State Department? U.S. Information Service? I haven't seen you around before. Did your parents just move into the District?"

"We're just visiting," Callie said.

"Right," Frank added. "Just plain civilians from Bayport."

"Tourists?" Ansel's tone of voice made the word sound as if he'd said "pond scum."

Joe faced off against the German kid. "Callie and Madeleine are old friends," he said. "They had a chance to get together here in Washington, and Callie wanted us to come with her. Is that a problem?"

"No problem," Maddy said quickly, grabbing Joe's arm. "Come on, the music is starting again. You must dance with me." She gave him that 150-watt smile. "After all, Callie told me she brought you with her because you're such a great dancer."

Frank and Callie joined Maddy and Joe, leaving Ansel to stand alone.

They danced for half an hour, then Maddy led them all back to the table where the diplomatic brat-pack was sitting. She introduced them quickly, rattling off names and countries. There was Willem, a doughy-looking Dutch guy with lank brown hair, and Stephanie, a cool blond girl whose father was someone fairly important in the

60

British embassy. Indira was an Indian girl with beautiful dark hair that reached her waist. She wore jeans, an expensive sweater, and a caste mark on her forehead. Joe didn't hear what country Tomas came from. He was tall and elegantly thin, with handsome dark looks.

Obviously, Ansel had already reported on them. The diplomatic brats greeted the Americans as if they'd just crawled out from under a rock.

Maddy, however, stayed with her American friends. She seemed almost defiant about it, keeping an arm around Joe as they stood by the table. That got her dirty looks from Ansel, Willem, and Tomas.

"So, Madeleine," Ansel said. Joe noticed that he pronounced her name perfectly. "Do you think you could get us invitations for the costume ball at your embassy this weekend? The one in honor of the Lafayette sword. I heard that your father is in charge of the display—"

Frank turned to Maddy. "Your father is in charge of the Lafayette sword?" he asked.

Madeleine barely looked at him as she yanked on Joe's arm. "This is my favorite song!" she exclaimed with another brilliant smile. The next second they were on the dance floor again. Joe could almost feel Ansel's and Frank's eyes boring into the back of his head.

They danced for three more songs—all of them

her favorites, Madeleine assured Joe. He couldn't help noticing, though, that they only returned to the table after Frank and Callie and Ansel and Indira had gotten up to dance.

They sat down even though the remaining diplomatic brats didn't bother to greet them. No one talked to them. Madeleine was determined to have a good time, anyway. She ordered fresh sodas for everyone and appetizers for the table. Joe decided that money was no problem for her.

Maddy made bright conversation, even though the other kids at the table didn't join in with her and Joe. Joe tried to keep up his part of the conversation, but it wasn't easy with all those hostile eyes shooting icy glares at him. When Ansel and Indira returned to the table, Joe could barely put up with the bad vibrations.

He breathed a sigh of relief as Frank and Callie rejoined them. "What do you say we move along?" Joe asked.

"Oh, you can't leave yet!" Madeleine said. "I wanted you to have a good time. To make up for—well, you know."

"It has been a pretty full day," Joe said. "We were all over the Mall, looking at museums—"

"Tourists," he overheard Indira saying to Ansel.

"And then we got jumped by some guy with a knife," Joe said, finishing his sentence.

"Jumped?" Tomas said, showing interest for

the first time. "You have to be careful in this city, you know."

Maddy, however, turned pale. "With a knife?" she echoed.

"Where did it happen?" Indira asked.

"Would you believe Capitol Hill?" Joe told her.

"I don't believe you," Ansel said bluntly. "But if you want to go home, go."

He became nasty, however, when Maddy got up as well. "We just treated you to a round of sodas," he said.

Joe sighed. "Look, we don't want any trouble. Why don't I pay?" He reached for his wallet—and found nothing in his back pocket. His face became red as he checked his other pockets and turned up nothing. "My wallet—I've lost my wallet!"

"Sure," Ansel told him, rising to his feet. "If you want to sponge off us—"

"Hey, pal, I don't—"

Ansel cut off Joe's words with a sharp shove to his shoulder.

All of a sudden a bouncer appeared at Joe's side, and the manager of the club was beside Ansel. "I want no problems," the manager said, smiling through gritted teeth.

"I'll take care of it," Frank said, throwing some money on the table.

Ansel swept the bills away. "I've come here

for months with no problem. Now you have the manager after us.''

''You do have a problem, champ,'' the manager told him. ''I want you out of here—now. All of you. Pick up your money,'' he said to Frank, then turned back to Ansel. ''As for you, I've had it with you and your friends. You're eighty-sixed.''

''What is eighty-sixed?'' Ansel demanded.

''You and your friends aren't welcome to come here anymore,'' the manager said.

Ansel's face turned a dull red. ''Do you know who my father is?''

''I don't really care,'' the manager told him with a shrug. ''There are lots more like you out there.''

Ansel was about to swing at the manager when the bouncer took him by the shoulder. ''This way,'' the big, beefy guy said. With that hand clamped onto him, there was nothing Ansel could do but let the bouncer march him off. Ansel's diplomatic brat friends trailed along.

The Hardys, Callie, and Madeleine left a minute later. ''Maddy, I'm sorry how this turned out,'' Callie said. ''I don't think your friends—''

''They weren't my friends,'' Madeleine told her. ''I just met them tonight—real snobs, wouldn't you say?''

''Well, I'm glad we're out of there,'' Joe said. He was trying to cool down, but his angry feelings showed in his long strides. He was crossing the street in the middle of the block way ahead of the others. "That Ansel—"

His voice was cut off by the roar of a car engine. The Porsche convertible he'd admired earlier was speeding down the street.

Joe saw the blond hair and knew Ansel was behind the wheel. He had the car set on a collision course with Joe.

Chapter

8

THE STEAMY AIR softened the outlines of the onrushing Porsche, making it seem almost ghostly. Joe knew that it was no phantom heading for him, though. If Ansel hit him, he'd be dead.

Joe swung his arms behind him, sending Madeleine, Callie, and Frank staggering backward. Then Joe dove and rolled to the far side of the street.

The Porsche missed him by inches.

Frank ran over to help Joe up. As he did, Ansel was throwing his Porsche screaming into reverse, not caring who got hit now. Joe and Frank were on one side of the street, the girls on the other.

Ansel angled his car up onto the sidewalk where Callie and Maddy were. Joe knew he had to do something to turn Ansel away from the girls.

He ran back into the street, yelling, "Hey, stupid, over here."

Ansel obliged and began a three-point turn. Joe hopped back up onto the sidewalk for a few steps, then dashed into the street again. The Porsche's tires screamed as Ansel completed the turn and sent the car rocketing forward again.

Got to get him away from the others, Joe thought as he zigzagged down the street. The roaring of the engine and the squealing of the tires were deafening. But even over the noise, Joe could hear Ansel's diplomatic brat-pack friends yelling encouragement for their driver. Screaming for blood—really nice guys, he thought.

The block he was running down looked as if it hadn't been touched in the last century. Solid row houses built of dark bricks formed ranks on either side of the street. They appeared quietly elegant behind their cast-iron fences and gardens.

However, the screeching of the diplomatic brats plus the engine roar of the car were neither quiet nor elegant. Lights began appearing in windows and then silhouettes of people. With luck, someone will call the cops, Joe told himself. All I have to do is survive till then.

Of course, these kids would claim diplomatic immunity. Joe hoped Lieutenant Grant would find some way to give them a hard time.

He reached a corner and glanced at the street sign. Church Street, one way. If he crossed over and went up that block, Ansel couldn't follow him.

Joe took a deep breath and started up the one-way street.

Ansel was past caring about traffic laws. He whipped the Porsche in a tight turn and sent it fishtailing up the narrow street and after Joe. A car was coming down, and for a moment it looked as if they would crash head-on into each other. At the last second, the other car swerved and ended up with two wheels on the sidewalk.

Ansel had slowed down for a second, but the moment the obstruction was out of the way, he flew past.

Joe hopped up on the sidewalk, and suddenly the immediate area around him was brightly lit. He glanced over his shoulder—and nearly stopped in shock. Ansel had pulled his car onto the sidewalk.

The car kept coming. Joe looked forward and noticed the knot of pedestrians moving his way. They were teenage girls, busy talking among themselves. They hadn't noticed what lay ahead on the sidewalk.

Joe tore down the long block, legs aching, lungs burning, yelling, "Watch out! This guy is a maniac!"

The girls stopped, gawked, then ran for safety. Joe was amazed he wasn't dead yet.

Then he realized Ansel had only been playing

with him. He could have taken Joe out whenever he wanted. The Porsche roared with new power. Joe glanced to the side and took the only chance he had. Grabbing the top of a cast-iron fence, he swung himself up and over to land in a private garden.

Ansel screeched by as Joe landed—right on top of a rosebush. Joe winced as he pushed himself up on wobbly weak legs, totally worn out. His outfit was ruined, thanks to all the thorns that had cut into his clothes. Of course, he would have looked a lot worse if Ansel had nailed him.

Joe took a few long, shaky breaths and leaned against the cast-iron fence, checking down the block for the Porsche. Its brake lights had come on, and a moment later, Joe heard rapid footsteps moving toward him. He went to one knee, and tried to remain hidden in the shadows.

"Which house was it?" Tomas's voice floated out of the darkness. "I think it was this one," he said, scaling the fence.

He was actually standing over Joe before he realized it. "Hey! He's here! Over here!" Tomas yelled.

Joe lurched to his feet, bringing his fist straight up from the ground. He didn't have Ansel's Porsche to hit Tomas with, but he did have the advantage of surprise. Joe's punch took Tomas right on the chin. He reeled back, then sat down hard.

Before Tomas could say anything more, Joe was up and swinging over the fence. He dashed across the street.

This could work out, he thought. Maybe I can lose these clowns.

"He's crossed the street, doubling back!" a voice cried from behind him. Willem's voice.

Regretting only that he didn't have a chance to punch out the Dutch kid as well, Joe broke into a shambling run.

Before he'd reached the corner again, Ansel had turned the Porsche around. Willem was running along Joe's side of the street. Joe could hear the footsteps on the pavement behind him. Across the street, judging by the noise, Tomas had gotten back on his feet and had joined Willem in the pursuit.

This old-fashioned neighborhood had large trees. Their branches cut out a lot of light from the street lamps and the moon. Joe felt as if he were running down a long tunnel with nothing at the end. His heart was pounding, his lungs burned, and his legs felt as heavy as lead. To top it off, pricks from that stupid rosebush stung. He was trying his best, but there was no way he could outrun a Porsche.

Joe knew he was fading fast. He'd be dead soon.

However, as he made his way down the street,

he found his brother standing in the middle of the road.

"Hey, Ansel," the older Hardy called, "stop picking on my kid brother."

Joe had to smile at that.

Ansel's answer, however, was to stomp on the gas. Joe started in horror as the Porsche shot out, dead on target for Frank.

Hopping up and down curbs hadn't been good for the car. As it roared toward them, its muffler trailed along the pavement, sending out showers of sparks. The effect was like that of a rocket set to search and destroy.

Frank stood still and faced the onrushing car, a confident smile on his face. At the last possible second, he leaped aside, landing on his shoulder in a roll that brought him immediately back to his feet.

Ansel frantically hit the brakes. He'd been so interested in smearing Frank, he'd forgotten a very important fact.

They were on a dead-end street. The Porsche was heading straight for an old-fashioned, cast-iron light pole.

Ansel's yell was drowned out by the screech of brakes. Then came the sickening crunch of a fender crumpling on the light pole. Nobody in the car appeared to be hurt, but there would be a few thousand dollars' worth of damage to the Porsche. Willem and Tomas ran to help their friends.

71

Frank appeared at Joe's side, taking his elbow. "Let's get out of here while they're distracted," he said.

"I think they'll have more distractions in a minute," Joe said. From the distance came the sound of sirens. He laughed as he and Frank hustled off. "Even if they get away from the cops, they'll have to pay plenty to get that fender fixed. By the way, Frank, thanks for handling them so neatly."

Frank grinned back. "Hey, what are big brothers for?"

Callie and Madeleine were waiting around the corner and halfway down the next block. "You were wonderful—both of you!" Maddy said, throwing her arms around the Hardys. "But I feel so bad, making trouble for you again."

"You can't blame yourself for this, Maddy," Callie said. "Joe just happened to lose his wallet, that's all."

"If I hadn't insisted on taking you to the Quarter, there would have been no trouble at all." Madeleine looked at her friends. "I don't know about you, but all of a sudden, I'm starving. Why don't we stop for a snack." She grinned at them. "My treat, but *you* pick the place."

They finally found a burger restaurant and took over a back booth. After a soda and something to eat, Joe began to feel human again. Maddy ordered an extra glass of seltzer and dipped a napkin in it, dabbing at Joe's face. "You have scratches on your cheek," she said, concerned.

"Yeah, but you should see the rosebush I landed on," Joe said with a laugh.

"You didn't come out of this unscathed, either," Callie said to Frank, pointing at his shoulder. "Trust you to roll through the only oil patch on that street."

Frank looked at the greasy smear on his shoulder. "This is going to take more than some seltzer," he said unhappily. "I'll see what I can do in the men's room."

"I'll walk you partway," Callie said with a grin. "I'm heading for the ladies'." She asked Madeleine, "Do you want to come along?"

Maddy shook her head, looking at her watch. "It's getting late. Suppose I pay our bill. Then, when you come out, we can all leave."

"Sounds good to me," Frank said, leaving the table.

After Madeleine got the check, she carefully began to count out the money to pay for it. Joe smiled, watching her serious face as she left a small pile of singles for the tip.

Then his smile disappeared. He recognized one of those singles. It was an old friend—the Worst Bill in the World. The last time he'd seen it, the bill had been in his wallet.

So what was Madeleine doing with it now?

Chapter

9

JOE'S HAND SHOT OUT, catching Madeleine in midcount. He had to force himself not to grip the girl's wrist too hard, but he wanted a good look at that dollar bill.

Maddy froze, staring at him.

"So, tell me, Maddy," Joe said, his voice mild but ice-cold. "Did you hold on to my wallet as well? Or did you just throw it away and keep my money?"

"W-what?" she asked in total shock. The dollar in her hand dropped to the table.

"It's plain bad luck." Joe shook his head at Maddy, pretending to sympathize. "Most people wouldn't recognize a bill that had been in their hip pocket even if you waved it under their noses."

The words came out as if his chest were being slowly squeezed. "But I had a dollar in my wallet that was the crummiest thing I'd ever seen. I mean, that buck was worn and about as limp as toilet paper. It also had a coffee stain, right over George Washington's face. Made George look like he had a big, brown mustache."

His finger tapped the bill on top of the pile Madeleine had been counting out. It landed right on the ring over Washington's face. "In fact, it looked just like this one. How do you explain that, Maddy?"

Madeleine seemed to shrink into herself. When she looked up at Joe again, her eyes shone with tears. "It *is* my fault after all," she said, her voice quavering as she dug around in her bag. "Here."

She pulled out Joe's wallet, then handed over what was left of his cash. Then she grabbed his hand in both of hers. "Joe, please don't tell Frank and Callie. *Please!*"

"Why not?" Joe's face was set in a cold, hard stare.

"It was all a mistake—a stupid mistake," Maddy said feverishly, begging him to under-stand. "My father was very angry about what happened at the store. He didn't give me permis-sion to go out tonight. I wasn't supposed to leave the house for a week."

"You were grounded?" Joe said.

Maddy nodded her head vigorously. "Yes. Grounded. I had to sneak out."

She looked at him as if that should explain everything. "There was no way I could get any money for the evening. I met Ansel and his friends outside, and they got me into the Quarter. Ansel started paying all sorts of attention to me. He ordered everything for me, telling me my money was no good with him around." Maddy shrugged her shoulders. "I—I let him, so I didn't have to worry about paying."

Her grip tightened on Joe's hand. "But I was supposed to be treating you, my friends. How was I going to do that without any money? Especially since I had invited you to make up for everything."

Madeleine used one hand to wipe a tear from her cheek. "Then I found the wallet under our table. It was the answer to a prayer. I thought all my problems were over. If I'd known it was yours, Joe—if I'd known how much trouble it would cause . . ."

Maddy's words ran down as Joe's gaze bored into her. His eyes were like chips of blue ice as he stared at her. It was the look a scientist would give to an unpleasant but interesting specimen.

"Nice try," Joe said, his voice mildly impressed. "You really should consider becoming an actress—that is, if you fail at your first career as a thief."

"But, Joe—I—you don't—" Madeleine floundered for words, thrown off balance by Joe's chilly response to her story.

"I should have figured it out before," Joe said. "It was obvious on the videotape from the store security camera. I ought to have spotted it back in the police station."

Maddy was staring at him now, her face pale. "S-seen what?"

"You used the same technique on me that you used with Callie. You jumped around and kept throwing your arm around me, getting me used to your touch—just like you did with Callie. Of course, with her, you used it to slip something into her pocket. With me, you slipped something out—my wallet."

He kept his gaze leveled on her. "You're a skilled dip, aren't you, Maddy—a professional pickpocket."

Her fingers left his hand as if it had turned red-hot.

"I can't imagine how a diplomat's daughter would pick up a skill like that. Picking pockets is something you're taught, not born with." He gave her a sour smile. "Besides, diplomats are usually better liars than thieves."

Madeleine sat huddled on the other side of the table. "I—I learned it from this girl I knew in Paris. She was—her name was Nadine—she was a street kid, working for a ring of pickpockets."

The words tumbled out of Madeleine now, like water that had been dammed up and suddenly broken loose. "We used to—I guess you'd say, hang out, sometimes. She had many crazy stories. Then she taught me how to do it."

She looked up at Joe with tear-filled eyes. "It started out as a joke, that's all. I was good at picking pockets. Very good. Nobody even knew when I did it—only Nadine."

"So, since you got away with it, you just kept it up." Joe's voice was cold.

"You don't understand!" Maddy's voice shook. "It's like a sickness. Sometimes I can't control it. I have this talent that I'm not supposed to use. Sometimes, when I'm happy or nervous, I forget."

Madeleine buried her face in her hands. "Oh, I wish I'd never learned it!" she whispered fiercely. "All it's done is get my friends into trouble."

She looked up pleadingly. "And if my father finds out—it will kill him. Papa works so hard at the foreign office. Any kind of scandal will wreck his career."

Madeleine's teary eyes begged Joe for help. "I think that's why he decided to bring us to America. He was afraid that I was hanging around with the wrong crowd back home."

She choked back a sob. "Poor Papa. He didn't know it was already too late."

Joe looked uncertainly at the French girl. Her tears seemed real, but he had a suspicion that they came as readily as her brilliant but phony smiles. "So what do you want from me?" he demanded.

"Don't tell your brother or Callie or my parents about—what I can do." Maddy shuddered with fear, then looked up at him with feverish eyes. "I'll make it up to you—I swear—I'll do anything."

Her fingers clutched at his hand again. But Joe shook her off. "Cool it. Frank and Callie are coming back."

"So," Frank said as he strolled up to the table. "Are we all set?"

"Maddy's just taking care of the tip," Joe said. "Guess what? We found my wallet. It must have fallen out of my pocket when we were at that club."

"Where did you find it?" Callie asked.

"Would you believe in Maddy's bag?" Joe answered with a grin.

That got a laugh from the other two. Maddy gazed at Joe with gratitude in her eyes.

They decided to walk back to Maddy's house and drop her off before heading for their hotel. As the foursome strolled down the street, it quickly broke into two couples—Frank and Callie in the lead, Joe and Madeleine bringing up the rear.

Maddy put an arm around Joe's waist and snuggled into his side as they walked along the quiet street.

"What are you going for now?" Joe asked. "My spare change?"

Madeleine leaped away from Joe as if he'd given her a megavolt electric shock. "I was—I just wanted to show how grateful I was." She stumbled over the words, her eyes going wide. "I thought you were being nice to me," she said in a small voice.

They stood for a long moment on the sidewalk looking at each other. "Maybe I'm being too nice to you," Joe finally said.

He was frowning, the troubled frown of a person who's not sure he's doing the right thing.

"I don't know if I can trust you, Maddy," Joe said slowly. "And once you lose somebody's trust, it's hard to earn back."

Madeleine sighed. "I'll just have to do my best," she finally said. "Come on, let's catch up with Frank and Callie."

It wasn't easy for Joe. Sore muscles in his legs screamed in protest when he picked up the pace. He was still aching from playing hide-and-seek with Ansel's Porsche.

As they headed down the street, Maddy took Joe's hand in hers. "At least you'll know where one of my hands is," she said with a ghost of a smile.

Joe knew he was supposed to laugh, but the laughter just wouldn't come.

They had cut the gap between themselves and the others to half a block when Madeleine suddenly froze, her fingernails digging into Joe's hand.

"That parked car we just passed," she whispered, her voice hoarse. "There's a man in it—with a gun!"

Chapter

10

As Joe Hardy turned back to see the car, he was momentarily blinded by the sudden glare of headlights. The car was moving now—it had pulled from the curb.

Up ahead of him were Frank and Callie, unaware that a car with an armed man inside might be following them.

Ignoring the stiffness in his aching legs, Joe forced himself into a shambling run down the nearly deserted street.

I'm probably overreacting. I never actually saw the gun, he thought. He couldn't stop himself from running to warn Callie and Frank, though. Must be a reaction to being chased by Ansel.

Luckily, the car was barely gliding along. As it pulled level with Joe, he could see the bulky outline of a guy leaning out the passenger-side window. Joe couldn't make him out clearly, but the MAC-10 submachine gun cradled in the guy's hands was impossible to miss.

The guy hadn't noticed Joe. He must have had all his attention on Frank and Callie. Unfortunately, the car had almost caught up with Callie and Frank by then.

"Watch out!" Joe yelled. "Get down!"

The guy in the car shot a look back at Joe, then took direct aim at him.

Joe dived for cover behind a parked van as half the MAC-10's clip whistled through the space where his chest had just been.

The muzzle flash from the gun lit up the gunman's face for an instant. Joe recognized the mismatched features of Old Ugly, the guy who'd tried to knife Callie in the Capitol.

Then the instant was past. Joe was behind the van, landing hard. He lay flat on the ground for a moment, the wind knocked out of him.

He heard another chattering burst of death from the MAC-10. Old Ugly must be emptying the gun's clip at Frank and Callie!

The sound of gunfire abruptly cut off and was replaced by the noise of an engine being revved and the squeal of tires as the car took off.

Joe forced himself to his feet and set off at a slow run for where he'd last seen Callie and

Frank. There they were, lying flat on the pavement. No blood—they were all right.

A second later they got shakily to their feet. Both were pale, but neither had been hit. They'd had a close call, but close doesn't count for hit men.

"Are you guys okay?" Joe asked.

"If we hadn't gotten your warning, we'd look like Swiss cheese," Callie said, shuddering. "Thanks, Joe."

"I was just carrying the message," Joe said. "Maddy's the one who spotted the guy in the car. Isn't that right, Maddy?"

He looked over his shoulder, but Madeleine wasn't standing there. In fact, she didn't appear to be on the block anymore.

Joe felt a cold chill run up his back. Had the gunmen gotten Maddy?

No, she wasn't on the sidewalk. She wasn't anywhere nearby. The car hadn't stopped to abduct her, either. No one else was around. Madeleine had just taken off after warning him. Joe shook his head. Should he thank her? Or was he trusting Madeleine too much?

Frank, Joe, and Callie took the fastest route back to their hotel. When they arrived on their floor, Frank took the key to Callie's room.

Motioning to the other two to stay away, he leaned against the wall, extending his arm to unlock the door while staying out of the doorway itself.

As the key clicked in the lock, he threw the door open, flattening himself against the wall again.

No shots rang out. In fact, nothing happened.

Frank went into a crouch and swung around the door to take a quick look inside the room. Then he shrugged and stood up. "Looks empty to me," he said.

Callie shook her head. "Don't you think you're taking things a little far?" she asked.

Joe shrugged. "You've never seen him when the family comes home from a long vacation."

"Hey, we were just shot at by a bozo who meant business," Frank said. He stepped back into Callie's room. "That reminds me—I'd better check for bombs or bugs."

A couple of minutes later Frank came back into the hall. "As far as I can see, the place is clean. Come on in, guys—we've got some stuff to talk about."

Joe took a quick trip down the hall to get some cans of soda, then they all settled down for a council of war.

"We've only been in this city for two days, and a lot of weird stuff has gone down," Frank said.

"That's putting it mildly," Joe said.

Callie nodded, ticking off the incidents on her fingers. "We've got a purse snatching, and the shoplifting accusation by the store manager. Then there's that pushing scene in the Metro—first me, then Joe—"

"Not to mention those guys following us at the Mall," Joe added.

"Ending with the guy and his knife in the Capitol," Callie went on. "Do we count Joe's fight at the club, that Ansel guy trying to run us down, and the Roaring Twenties–style rubout on the way home?"

She looked down at her fingers. "That's eight separate bits of trouble since we got here. Boy, time really flies when you're having a great time."

Joe shook his head and looked at his brother. "Who told me this was going to be a nice, quiet vacation?"

Frank wasn't in a mood for joking. "We've walked into the middle of something here, something dangerous. The only way to get out of this alive is to find out what's going on. That was why I wanted to go to the Quarter tonight."

"Well, I knew you had to have another reason," Joe said.

"Did it help?" Callie asked.

Frank shook his head. "I'm not sure," he admitted. "But I have noticed something. We can break down all the incidents of the past couple of days into two categories. There's the purse snatching, the pushing on the platform, the tails, the guy with the knife—''

''And the guy with the gun,'' Joe cut in. ''Did either of you notice that he was the same guy who followed us into the Capitol?''

Frank stared at his brother for a second. ''Are you sure?'' Then he shook his head. ''That ties it up a little closer.''

Callie and Joe looked at him in confusion.

''Don't you see?'' Frank said. ''Five incidents dealing with complete strangers—and all, it seems, aimed at Callie.''

''*What?*'' Callie sat up straighter on the couch.

''Sorry, Callie, but look at the facts.'' Frank's face wasn't happy as he tried to convince his girlfriend. ''It was your purse that got snatched. You were the first guy's target on the Metro platform. Joe was attacked only when he took off after the guy.''

''You can't blame those guys following us at the Mall on me,'' Callie said.

''We don't know who they were following,'' Frank admitted. ''But when the guy with the knife finally attacked us, he went for you.''

''And when he came back with a gun, he went for you and Frank, not me and Maddy.'' Joe frowned. ''This is getting a little scary.''

''You're telling *me*,'' Callie said with a gulp. She looked at Frank. ''Why is this happening?''

''I keep remembering Old Ugly talking to his

friends back at the Capitol," Frank said. "I caught two words—'*le coup*.'"

"Sounds French," Joe said, frowning. "But I don't think these guys look like they're involved in a military coup."

"It means other things in French, too, you know," Callie said. "It could be a blow." She shuddered. "Like a knife blow. Or a shot."

"Or a criminal job," Frank added. "Maybe we've gotten in the way of a gang."

"Great." Callie rolled her eyes. "But you said there were two categories of incidents."

"You're not going to like this any better," Frank said. "We've got the shoplifting incident, where Maddy got you in trouble. Then there was the run-in at the club." He looked sharply at Joe. "Are you sure you simply lost that wallet?"

Joe stiffened. "What do you mean?"

"We all saw that videotape from the store. Maddy is pretty light with her fingers." Frank leaned over his brother. "Could she have gotten it out of your pocket?"

"No way," Joe told him. Even as he spoke, he wondered why he was protecting Maddy. Maybe it was a hunch, but he thought he'd get more out of her alone than siccing Frank and Callie on her as well.

Frank's gaze was still leveled on Joe, but he didn't keep up his questioning. "Well, anyway, Maddy was responsible in part for that whole scene—and involved in what came after,'' he finally said.

"So we've got five things that are strangers' faults and three that are Maddy's." Callie rubbed a hand over her face, suddenly looking very tired. "I just don't understand. We've been writing letters back and forth for years. I really thought I knew Maddy. Here was my chance to meet her, and I was so excited."

She flung herself back on the couch, scowling. "Some excitement. My friend gets me in trouble, and people are trying to kill me. It doesn't make any sense. The Madeleine Berot who wrote all those letters is nothing like the girl we've met. She's gone through a complete change of personality—it's like she's another person." Callie sighed. "She really had me fooled."

"She isn't all bad," Joe pointed out. "She really seemed sorry when she got you in trouble, and she did warn us about that guy with the gun."

Frank looked grim. "The only reason Callie's in this city is Madeleine Berot."

"It could be two separate cases, or two separate gangs," Frank continued, deep in thought. "The question is, what does anyone want?"

"Well, I know what I want," Callie spoke up suddenly. "That's the key to your room. All of a sudden I don't feel very safe sleeping in here."

Frank got out his key. "It's yours—just as soon as we check for any possible surprises."

The room next door was clean, too, and Callie moved in.

"You know what to do now?" Frank asked at the door.

Callie nodded, reciting Frank's instructions like a schoolchild who's memorized them. "Keep the door locked, and don't let people in unless they're accompanied by a Hardy." She grinned, staring hard at Frank and Joe. "Just memorizing your faces."

"Hilarious," Frank said sourly. "Please, Callie, be careful."

"Okay."

Frank stood outside the door as Callie doublelocked it, then put on the bolt. Then he headed for Callie's room, where he and Joe would stay.

"Think we'll have any unfriendly visitors tonight?" Joe asked.

Frank growled in response as he settled down for sleep.

Joe lay under the covers but couldn't drift off.

Neither, it seemed, could Frank. He quietly slipped out of bed, picked up a chair in the darkness, and brought it over to the door, where he jammed it under the knob and sat on it. He had scoffed at Joe's suggestion earlier.

But now Frank Hardy was taking no chances.

Chapter

11

A HEAVY HAND landed on Frank Hardy's shoulder, brutally shaking him out of his uneasy sleep.

Instantly, Frank was awake—if not very aware. He took a wild swing at the fuzzy figure in the murk in front of him, nearly falling to the floor. The shaker jumped back as if he'd just awakened a wild man.

Maybe he had.

"Wha-whazzat?" Frank said, trying to figure out why he was sitting in a chair. This wasn't his room at home. It was a hotel room. Callie was next door—maybe in danger!

"You sure you're awake?" Joe asked a little skeptically.

Frank calmed down. "Yeah. I'm awake and hurting." He stretched, rubbing his back.

"Chairs are not constructed for sleeping in. But I'm sure you didn't shake me to get a furniture report. What's up?"

"I was lying here, wide awake, and I had an idea," Joe explained.

Frank fixed him with the evil eye. "You woke me after I'd finally fallen asleep to tell me you had an idea?"

"It's early morning," Joe said. "And that ties in with my idea." He explained what he had in mind while Frank went into the bathroom and threw some cold water on his face.

Awake at last, Frank studied his brother. "That actually does make sense," he finally admitted. "But I'm going to make *you* go over and wake up Callie and explain it to her." He looked around for a clock. "What horrible hour is it, anyway?"

"Six-thirty," Joe said. "We'll have to move if we really want to catch them. You get Callie, and I'll try to wash the sleep out of my head," Frank said as a yawn popped his jaw open, startling him. "I think this is no time to get up during vacation."

Forty minutes after Joe had awakened Frank, he, Joe, and Callie were standing under the awning of an apartment house. The three of them were across the street and down the block from where the Berots lived.

Callie hid a yawn behind her hand as they stood

watching the Berots' door. "You want to explain this to me one more time?" she said.

"Frank started me thinking last night," Joe began.

Callie gave him a look. "I'm glad something started you," she said.

Joe ignored her, going on. "Frank blamed one set of awful stuff on strangers, and the other on Madeleine Berot. We can't check up on the mystery men, but we can check up on the Berots. There are three of them, and three of us."

"So we're hanging around here at this ungodly hour so we can follow them when they come out," Callie finished. "What do you think we'll find out?"

Joe shrugged. "I don't know, but it's better than being sitting ducks."

"You got me there," Callie admitted. "Okay, who gets which Berot?"

"I'm following Maddy," Joe quickly announced, getting a shake of the head from Callie.

"Trust you to follow the girl," she told him. "Are you sure you aren't falling for her?"

"Falling? No way," Joe answered. But there are things I want to talk to her about, he said to himself.

"I'd like to tail Mr. Berot," Frank said, "if that's okay with you, Callie."

"Sure," Callie said. "That leaves Mrs. Berot for me—or should I call her Madame?" She grinned. "I think you guys are sticking me with the easiest tail job because I have the least experience in following people."

Frank and Joe both held their breaths, expecting an explosion.

"Actually, that's probably a good idea. Thanks for thinking ahead, guys."

The Hardys remained in astonished silence for a good half-hour before Mr. Berot emerged from the building, dressed in a suit.

"Here's my guy," Frank said. "Wish me luck." He waited until Mr. Berot had half a block on him, then started strolling after him.

Joe glanced at his watch. "Frank may have a more boring job than he thinks. Mr. Berot's probably on his way to work."

"Well, then, I guess he'll have to plant himself in front of the French embassy," Callie said. "You can never tell when Mr. Berot might pop out for some sort of funny business." She grinned. "I expect he gets a lunch hour and a couple of coffee breaks."

How much longer would they have to wait there? Joe wondered.

Not much, as it turned out.

"Joe," Callie whispered, grabbing his arm. "Look."

A blond woman stepped out of the building, wearing a navy blazer and a gray skirt.

"That's Mrs. Berot—my turn," Callie said.

As Joe turned to look, the woman across the street glanced at her watch, then rubbed her hands together in a nervous gesture. He remembered that from his introduction to the woman. She'd rubbed her hands the same way when Frank and her husband got into that very undiplomatic argument.

Callie let the woman pass, then set off after her. "Wish me luck, Joe."

"Good luck," Joe said dutifully. You'll probably need it, he added silently.

Joe settled back to wait for Madeleine. She didn't show—apparently taking a nice, long rest after the night's dancing and running around.

Joe looked at his watch for the hundredth time and shook his head. I could have slept for another two hours, he told himself, shifting his weight from one foot to the other.

At last, however, his waiting was rewarded. The apartment house door swung open, and there was Maddy. Joe stepped back into the shadows of the awning, allowing her to get a lead on him.

He let Maddy get well ahead—no use taking a chance that she'd see him tailing her. And he certainly didn't have to run to keep up. Wherever Madeleine was going, she was heading there at a very easy pace.

Joe followed as Maddy strolled down to M Street. He remembered there was a bridge over the gorge between Washington proper and

Georgetown up there. Sure enough, that's where Madeleine was heading.

Time to close up the gap, Joe told himself. There are lots of winding little streets in Georgetown. We had a case where someone almost lost us there.

At least the streets weren't jammed. Maddy stayed to the main shopping areas on M Street.

Joe sighed as she started hitting the boutiques. Hope she doesn't get popped for shoplifting again, he thought. I don't know how the cops would react to my staking out the station house.

For the next hour and a half, Madeleine went from shop to shop, trying things on and checking things out. Generally, she spent about twenty minutes per store. So, when she was in one for half an hour, Joe began to get a little concerned.

What if there's a back entrance I don't know about? he wondered.

Finally he abandoned the observation post he'd taken up across the street by a stationery store and went to look in the window.

There was Maddy—standing right in front of him at the checkout counter.

Joe ducked down and headed across the street to hide in the entrance of an old-fashioned pharmacy. Just my luck to peek into the first store where she buys something, he groused. Hope she didn't see me.

Madeleine came out of the boutique and set off down the street without checking for any tails— and without a glance in Joe's direction.

He stayed on the opposite side of the street from her and nearly a block behind. Maddy didn't seem suspicious at all. She was just walking along, obviously very pleased with herself and her window-shopping.

She walked up to a pay phone, put in some coins, and started punching in a number. Taking advantage of the distraction, Joe moved closer. He slipped into a candy store on her side of the street and watched Madeleine through the panes of the front window. She seemed to be making notes on a copy of a guidebook.

"Get you something, son?" the elderly owner asked.

A few minutes later, armed with a small bag of peppermint sticks, Joe took off after Maddy as she walked along Wisconsin Avenue.

He sighed through another boring round of window-shopping. Then Maddy suddenly left the main street, turning right on Q Street.

Joe remembered that there was another bridge back into Washington proper up ahead—as well as a bunch of embassies.

Maddy had reached the pair of massive buffalo statues that flanked the end of the bridge. There was a sharp curve, and for a moment Joe lost sight of her. He picked up his pace.

Out of the corner of his eye, Joe saw a car move up. He didn't think about it because he was so interested in seeing where Madeleine had gone.

Before he got four more steps, though, the car suddenly swerved off the road to block the sidewalk right in front of him.

Joe took a step back as three guys burst out of the car. He recognized two of them. One was the short, stocky guy who'd followed them around the Mall. The other was the tall, thin one who'd tried to push Callie—then him—off the station platform.

They tackled him like pros, Shorty and Skinny grabbing Joe's arms. While he tried to pull loose, the third, a pimply faced wiry guy, grabbed him by the legs.

Writhing and kicking, Joe struggled madly. It did him no good. He had no leverage to fight off his attackers. They had no trouble lifting him up to the stone railing of the bridge. Below him was a sixty-foot drop.

And these guys were ready to send him down it.

Chapter

12

FRANK HARDY WAS FROWNING as he trudged along after Henri Berot. They hadn't gone two blocks, and already things were weird.

If Berot did work at the embassy, he was heading in the wrong direction. For another, Berot was using all the classic tactics to spot and lose a tail—hardly the actions of an innocent man.

The tail-spotting maneuvers began as soon as Berot reached a corner with a red light. The Frenchman darted across in front of the traffic. Not the kind of behavior you'd expect from him, Frank told himself. He refused to give himself away by darting across, too.

Frank did, however, cut the distance between himself and his quarry as they walked for several blocks. That wasn't difficult, since the morning crowds had become thicker and thicker, giving Frank lots of cover. Berot walked on and on, seemingly with no destination in mind. He headed north, then east, then south, wasting more than an hour in aimless wandering.

At long last the Frenchman checked his watch and nodded to himself. Then he started walking at a serious pace—south, and then west. They entered a shopping district, full of hurrying commuters. Frank used the mass of people to shield himself from Elementary Tailing Trick Number Two—using the plate-glass store display windows as mirrors to check behind you. Berot kept on stopping to "window-shop" at store after store.

Once, Frank let the crowd carry him past Berot. Sheltered behind two guys and a young woman, all of them carrying briefcases, he wasn't noticed. Then he just moved with the crowd, keeping Berot in sight with the same window-shopping trick the Frenchman was using.

As they moved through the neighborhood, the crowd of commuters grew. Then, finally, everyone swirled underground—into the local Metro station. Standing by a newsstand, Frank let Berot go down ahead of him.

As he followed on the escalator, Frank frantically dug through his pockets. He sighed happily when he came up with the fare card Joe had bought for him. At least he wouldn't lose Berot at the machines.

Frank slipped his fare card through the turnstile three gates over and six people behind Henri Berot. He crouched a little, hiding his height in the crowd. He let the moving mass of people take him over to the escalators and down to the train platforms. Now was not the time to call attention to himself by pushing closer to his quarry.

He kept a sharp eye on where Berot was heading, however. The Frenchman got on a blue line Metro train, heading downtown. Frank got on the same train, one car away. He had a bit of a struggle keeping a position near the doors against the press of the other commuters. But he had to stay there. At each stop he had to make sure Berot didn't get off.

Two stops after boarding the train, Berot got off at Metro Center. So did Frank, but Berot didn't leave the platform. Then Frank remembered that this was a transfer point. They were stuck on the platform together. If Berot glanced over and recognized Frank, the whole gig would be ruined.   Frank was lucky. The French diplomat seemed more interested in checking his watch and looking down the tunnel where the train was expected. He didn't have any time to spare for his fellow commuters.

A red line train pulled in, and Berot got aboard. Then Berot pulled his antitail trick. He stepped onto the train, waited for a moment, then stepped off.

The tactic wasn't a new one for Frank. He was actually stepping off himself when a late commuter came racing through the doors, crashing into Frank and pushing him back inside.

Frank leaped for the doorway, throwing himself halfway through the closing doors. Then he struggled just as hard to pull himself back in. He'd just caught sight of Berot leaping into the next car. Apparently, after seeing nobody suspicious jumping onto the platform, the Frenchman had decided the train was safe and boarded it again.

Frank smiled for a moment in triumph, then frowned. There was a red line station much nearer to the Berots' building than the blue line station Berot had walked to. Every step of this journey had been designed to detect and discourage tails.

Two stops later, at Judiciary Square, Berot got off the train and stayed off. Frank followed the man up the escalator and onto the street, blinking for a moment as the morning sun reflected off an enormous building of brick and cream-colored stone ahead of him. For a second he nearly lost Berot in the rush-hour crowd.

Berot headed directly for the huge brick building, which had to be at least a hundred years old. Frank thought it might be some recently renovated office building. Instead, it turned out to be a museum of architecture—and the place was just opening.

Standing by the sign that identified the place, Frank hung back as Berot stepped briskly into the museum. Frank stood for a moment, trying to come to a decision. If he went charging in he could be spotted, and what if Berot was only using the place to shake anyone on his trail? He could be out a side door and lost forever in a couple of minutes.

Finally, taking a deep breath, Frank stepped into the dimly lit entryway. At the other end, he took a deeper breath, confronted with an enormous hall. The place was long enough to accommodate a couple of football fields and amazingly high. Enormous pillars supported the ceiling.

The worst thing from Frank's point of view, however, was that this vast place was empty of people. No way could he get near Berot. He did spot him off in the distance, glancing impatiently at his watch and gazing off at another entrance to the building.

He's waiting for someone, Frank realized. I need a better observation post.

That's when he noticed the series of arcades rising toward the ceiling. The place was built like the nineteenth-century version of a shopping mall, with a huge skylight and three floors of what—offices?—looking down on the central hall.

Frank decided if he could get up to the next floor, he'd be in the perfect place to observe Berot, without being seen.

He found his way to an elevator, which chugged its way slowly. As soon as he got off, Frank headed for the railing overlooking the vast hall below. A cement column even gave him cover.

Scanning the area below, Frank caught his breath. Someone was coming from the far end of the building, heading directly for Berot. The man wore a loud, European-cut sport coat and tight pants, and his head looked too small for his bull-like body. His skin was sallow, and even from his observation post, Frank could make out the pock-marks on the man's face. This was the guy who'd tried to knife Callie—and then tried to shoot her and Frank.

The two men surveyed the empty floor, then walked over to talk together.

Okay, Frank told himself. There is only one gang behind all of Callie's troubles.

As Berot and the ugly man spoke, however, Frank watched their gestures become shorter and more violent. He couldn't hear what they were saying, but from their expressions, they were having a disagreement. A serious disagreement.

Berot shook his head frantically. The big ugly

guy frowned, thumping Berot in the chest with a finger the size of a small cucumber. Frank had to admire Henri Berot for guts. He would hate to argue with a guy who could loom over him like that.

One gang, Frank decided. But if I'm not mistaken, there are two factions.

In spite of the way Berot argued, the other man apparently won the argument.

Berot seemed to deflate, then finally he shrugged his shoulders and shook his head. Even from his vantage point, Frank could see him saying, "Do what you want."

That was apparently all the big man had to hear. He abruptly turned and headed out of the museum.

Frank was caught off guard. Which one of them should he follow?

He decided on the big guy. Maybe he could find out where this man and his small army were heading out.

Frank dashed to the far end of the arcade and located a flight of stairs. He clattered down. With luck, he still might be able to catch up with the guy.

Hoping Berot wouldn't turn to see him, Frank ran for the far entrance. Just as he made it, the entranceway filled up with a mob of people. By the time Frank got through, the man was gone.

"First tour group of the day," a museum staffer told Frank.

Frank nodded grimly. His chance to link the attackers and the Berots had just disappeared into the city outside.

Chapter

13

IT'S MY LAST CHANCE, Joe Hardy thought as he struggled against his attackers. Twisting violently, he got one foot free and planted it in the chest of the man holding his legs. He kicked as hard as he could, and the pimply-faced thug went flying backward and fell flat across the sidewalk of the Buffalo Bridge.

Even without their friend's help, though, the two guys gripping his arms manhandled him so his feet were heaved over the concrete guardrail of the bridge. Joe grabbed frantically for the protruding lip of the concrete rail and held tight when the two strong arms let go of his arms. Rough concrete scraped against his fingers as the thugs kept pushing at him to make him fall.

Joe managed to pull himself up and lift one leg

over the rail to aim a glancing kick at the short, unshaven guy on his left. He flung his body up, trying to kick the other leg over, but in the process one hand lost its grip. The guy on his right tossed Joe's legs back over the rail. Now Joe was dangling by one hand fifty feet above an expressway and the rock-clogged waterway of a creek another ten feet below that and to the left.

"Ecoutez!" a high, shrill voice screamed. The arm pounding on Joe turned at the sound and forgot Joe. The voice now yelled, *"Les flics!"*

Joe didn't speak French, but he'd heard that phrase before. He also recognized the voice doing the screaming. It was Madeleine Berot!

The thugs looked at each other uncertainly for a moment, then dashed for their car, collecting the guy Joe had kicked.

Joe got a grip with his other hand and swung himself up and onto the bridge.

In seconds the thugs were all in the car, revving the motor and pulling away. Shorty, the guy with the unshaven face, leaned out a window. "Nadine," he yelled to Maddy, *"viens avec nous!"*

That sounded like, "Come with us!"

French words flew back and forth at lightning speed, a complete mystery to Joe.

As the siren came closer, Maddy frantically waved her arms. *"Allez! Allez!"*

Her gorilla friends pulled into a tight U-turn,

doubling back into Georgetown. Madeleine ran along the bridge back into Washington proper.

Joe scrambled to his feet and took off after Maddy. Before he'd gotten ten feet, however, he saw the source of the siren—it was an ambulance, blasting along on the expressway below him.

She'd have seen the ambulance from where she was standing, Joe thought as he started running again. She knew the cops weren't coming. That was a lie—a lie to save my life!

Maddy was far ahead of him now, tearing down the sidewalk as fast as she could. But Joe was the better runner, and he had strong motivation— curiosity. He had a lot of questions for this girl.

As he came up behind her, he called, "Hey, Nadine, why don't you just tell me the whole story?"

Maddy whirled, her eyes wide, bracing herself against the wall of a building. "I didn't know they were going to do that," she gasped out. "I called them when I realized you were following me, and they said for me to lead you to the bridge. I thought they would only try to scare you off—I didn't think they would try to kill you."

The flow of words slowed as the girl realized she had answered to the name *Nadine*. Her shoulders sagged and she slumped against the brick wall behind her.

"Come on," Joe said, taking her by the arm. "I'll introduce you to a new American custom."

He led Maddy back into Georgetown, to an ice-cream store they had passed. Sitting in a booth with ice-cream sodas in front of them, he suggested again that she talk. "And the whole truth this time, no stories. Let's start with your real name."

The girl took a deep breath. "It's Nadine—Nadine Rodier."

Joe nodded. "Cute. You used your own name for the girl who taught Madeleine Berot how to pick pockets." He studied her for a long moment. "I guess that's what you do for a living. So where's the real Maddy Berot?"

Nadine shook her head. "I don't know. We came over on the same plane. After her family left customs, they got into a car—driven by one of us. A few minutes later we came out and got into another car—one with their papers and luggage."

"I think I'm still missing a few steps," Joe said, shaking his head. "Maddy—I mean, Nadine—what's the whole idea?"

"You're right—I do pick pockets for a living." Nadine shrugged a little helplessly. "My parents left me with a gang when I was a little kid. The Old Man—that's what we called our boss—taught us to pick the pockets of the tourists. He got the money. If we didn't share, we got punished." She shivered a little. "About two months ago a man came to visit the Old Man. He showed him a picture. The Old Man looked at it, then called me over.''

Nadine took a sip of her soda, then continued. "I was scared that I'd done something wrong, but the Old Man said it would be all right. The man was renting me, to play a part in a scam. I was supposed to pretend to be his daughter.''

"So Henri Berot is a phony, too," Joe said.

"The whole family. The real Berots were picked up at the airport, and I haven't seen them since. Paul and Sylvie—those are their real names—just slipped into their identities. The real Monsieur Berot worked in Paris, and it seems no one in the embassy here knew him. Paul looked enough like Henri Berot to pass—just as I looked enough like the real Madeleine.''

"A whole family of fakes," Joe finally said. "Unbelievable. So what's the scam?''

Nadine shrugged again. "I don't know. I'm only here as window dressing. Paul—you met him as Monsieur Berot—is a professional thief, and he's supposed to steal something to do with the French embassy. I think Sylvie, the woman who's pretending to be my mother, is his assistant. I'm only here because they needed a teenage girl who looked like Madeleine.''

"What about the rest of the gang?" Joe asked.

"A strong-arm squad was sent to Washington ahead of us," Nadine said. "They kidnapped the real Berots. The leader is a man called La Bête—

the Beast." She shuddered. "He's a very ugly man."

"I think I've met him," Joe said grimly.

"He's been arguing with Paul, trying to take over the operation," Nadine explained. "When we found letters from a pen pal in Madeleine's things, and then learned that Callie was coming to Washington, La Bête wanted to kill her."

"He's certainly been trying hard enough."

Nadine nodded. "Paul wanted to try scaring her away with the purse snatching." She looked down. "Then I was supposed to be so obnoxious, she'd want to leave."

"I'd say you did a pretty good job of that," Joe told her.

"I thought it would be sort of fun," Nadine said in a small voice. "Madeleine had such nice things—things I never had. But I was stuck in the apartment all day. I didn't have a chance to enjoy anything. So when you turned up, I argued with Paul to let me go out with you. Then I'd be able to go shopping, and dancing—"

"And make fun of us and get us into trouble," Joe added.

"I can't expect you to believe me, but I do feel bad about what happened in the store and the club," Nadine said. "I was doing my job. But"— she looked up at Joe almost shyly—"I found myself liking you all, even if you are—how do you say it? Straight-arrows?"

Joe had to smile at that.

"I hated watching Callie cry as we went to the police station," Nadine said. "And then we found out that La Bête wasn't following Paul's orders—his people were trying to kill Callie. They tried to push her, then you, under a train, and you mentioned something that happened in the Capitol—"

"I think that was La Bête himself, trying to knife Callie," Joe said. "He was the one with the gun in the car last night, you know, when you warned us."

Nadine nodded. "He's like a mad bull. Me—I don't mind stealing. But killing . . ."

She shook her head.

Joe decided to press his advantage. "Come on, Nadine. Tell me about the theft Paul's going to pull."

She threw out her arms. "I really don't know."

"Okay. I won't ask you to help me find out, but I want you to *let* me find out," Joe told her. "Take me back to your apartment. If I find something that gives me a clue, fine. If not, you're off the hook." He gave her a sidelong look. "It's the least you can do. You almost got us killed, too, you know. Remember Ansel and his car."

"All right, all right," Nadine said. "I'll let you in—but only for a fast look."

Time seemed to crawl on the half-mile walk from the ice-cream shop to the building where

Nadine and the others were living. At last, however, they were entering the Berots' apartment. "Sylvie?" Nadine called into the hallway. "Paul?"

She glanced back at Joe, standing in the doorway. "They're not here," she said. "Go on— look around. Don't expect me to help you."

They reached the far end of the living room, Nadine following Joe. Then they heard the sound of a key in the lock of the door.

Her eyes wide with terror, Nadine grabbed Joe's arm and threw open a closet door. Together, they jumped inside and swung the door shut just as the outside door opened.

They heard footsteps—probably a man's—on the polished wood floor. Moving toward them. Then the phone rang.

The man stepped into the kitchen to answer it, and Joe heard superfast French. Nadine whispered a translation in his ear, almost inaudible over the arguing voice in the next room.

"It's Paul—he's talking with La Bête—getting a report on how they failed with you."

Paul had now reached the shouting stage.

"Paul says La Bête is getting us too much attention. I think La Bête is saying too many people are suspicious already. Paul's telling him to stop the attempts on you three—"

She suddenly drew in her breath. "Now La

Bête wants to get rid of the real Berots!'' she whispered.

More French followed, and Nadine's fingers gripped Joe's arm so tight, it hurt him. ''Paul says no—not until he finishes the job.''

Joe relaxed as the phony Mr. Berot finished his conversation, but Nadine maintained her painful grip on Joe's arm. Her voice was tight and strained when she spoke.

''The job,'' she whispered in a scared voice. ''It's tomorrow night—after that, they're dead.''

Chapter

14

Joe turned to Nadine, standing beside him in the darkness of the closet. "Do you mean—" he began, but she clamped a trembling hand over his mouth.

"Not so loud!" Her voice was a nervous hiss. "We don't want him to hear us."

They stood in silence for a moment, until Paul's footsteps receded into the distance. "He's in the rear bedroom now," Nadine said.

She eased the closet door open, peeking around it to check that the coast was clear. Silently, she beckoned Joe out of the closet. Then she shooed him out of the apartment.

"You've got to get out of here," Nadine told Joe outside in the hallway. "This whole situation is getting too dangerous for you.'' She dug in her bag.

"What are you doing?" Joe asked.

"Looking for the key," she explained. "In about two seconds I'll walk into the apartment, all innocence. I warned La Bête's people that the police were coming and ran away. I haven't seen you since, don't know anything about you, and don't *want* to know anything more."

Now it was Joe's turn to grab her arm. "And what about the people La Bête is holding? The real Berots?"

"Look, I don't want them to die," Nadine said. "But if the others find out I've been talking to you, *I'm* the one who'll get killed. Understand?"

"You hardly told me anything. What we've got to know is where the Berots are being kept." Joe's eyes bored into hers. "You said it yourself, Nadine. Stealing is one thing—killing is another. Are you going to let those people die?"

"I-I'll try to find out." Nadine glanced around, getting more and more nervous. "You can't stay here. If Sylvie turns up and sees you, I'm dead. Get it?"

She looked pleadingly at Joe's stubborn face. "How about this? I'll call you tonight—seven-thirty—with everything I've found out. Okay? But now you've got to go."

She pushed at his chest, and Joe finally left. As the door swung shut, his last view of Nadine showed her leaning beside her door, sighing in relief.

Joe sat by the phone that evening from seven-thirty until eight o'clock. Nadine never called.

Callie was sitting on the couch of the Hardys' hotel room. Frank paced the floor, looking at his brother every once in a while. "Okay, Joe, spill it. Why did you make us sit around here and stare at the phone with you. What's going on?"

"Time for a council of war," Joe finally said.

As Joe was sharing his information, Frank suddenly got up from the couch. "Okay, so the guy that Berot—"

"Paul," Joe corrected him.

"Whoever. The big ugly guy has to be La Whoozis—La Bête." Frank smiled grimly. "At least we have a name for the guy who's been trying to kill us. The question is, what sort of heist is his partner going to pull off tomorrow night?"

"I'm not sure what," Callie said abruptly, "but I think I know where it's going to go down. I followed Mrs. Berot, or Sylvie, to a costume shop today. Didn't one of those diplomatic brats mention a costume ball coming up this weekend?"

"That's right—something in honor of the Lafayette sword."

"Which Mr. Berot is supposed to be in charge of," Joe added.

"You don't think—" Callie said.

Joe shrugged. "There's only one way to find out."

The weather seemed a little cooler the next morning as Frank and Joe stepped into the chancery of the French embassy. The reception area of the office was a little disordered. A tall stack of gleaming white parchment envelopes leaned at a dangerous angle on the reception desk, where a young blond woman was slipping cards into them.

"Hey, she's cute," Joe said to his brother, loud enough to make the girl look up from her work.

Frank just took a deep breath. Was it hormones that made Joe act like an idiot sometimes? His younger brother was suddenly acting like the cool guy from situation comedies—the type who doesn't realize he's a real jerk.

"Seems a shame that a pretty girl like you has to work so hard on a Saturday morning," Joe said, resting both hands on the desk to lean over her.

The receptionist's green eyes inspected him for a moment as her hands continued to slip cards into envelopes, apparently working on autopilot. "These are last-minute invitations to a costume ball—"

"Right, right," Joe said, still looking into her

eyes. "Being held at the—the—" He snapped his fingers as if the answer were right on his tongue.

"The headquarters of the Continental Order. We are displaying the Sword of Lafayette at their museum."

"Sure—the Lafayette sword. Mr. Berot is in charge of that."

The blond girl nodded. "He's a member of the Continental Order. His great-great-great-great-great-grandfather was a navy officer who helped in your revolution. As the eldest son in his family, he belongs to the Continental Order. It shows how long the friendship between France and America has lasted."

"Of course," Joe said as if he were a member himself. "I guess this will be some party, huh? A chance to start all sorts of friendships."

"The ambassador will present the sword in a private ceremony, and then, on with the party." The girl frowned as she ran out of envelopes, and opened the desk drawer for more. She also glanced at the desk clock. "You're early, you know," she said.

Joe gave her a big smile and leaned closer. "Hey, I think I'm just in time. Tell me, have you got a date for this big hoedown?"

As he watched his brother grin expectantly, Frank suppressed an urge to throw up. If Joe pulled this one off, Frank knew he'd be hearing about it for years to come.

The girl behind the reception desk put her hand over her mouth. For a second Frank thought she was coughing. Then he caught the faintest sound of giggling. She was struggling not to laugh in Joe's face!

"I—I'm sorry," the girl finally managed to say, her cute little nose wrinkling as she fought to keep a straight face. "But you see, we have a rule here—we're not allowed to date the help."

Joe looked as if somebody had just socked him in the head with a hammer. "The—the help?" he stammered.

The girl stopped laughing now. "You're the messengers, yes? Here to pick up and hand-deliver the last-minute invitations?"

"Uh, no." Joe suddenly straightened up, mortified at being taken for a messenger boy. One arm knocked over the pile of envelopes stuffed with invitations.

Oh, great, Frank thought, having a hard time holding back his laughter, too. I'll never be able to tell this story, because Joe will die of embarrassment.

He held back, afraid to move as Joe scrambled to gather up the papers he'd knocked over. Joe picked some up, dropped them, then finally delivered a big, untidy bundle into the arms of the receptionist, who came around the desk to collect them.

Frank bit his lip, afraid he'd laugh out loud.

"No," the young woman said, looking into Joe's beet red face. "I guess you aren't a messenger."

"Actually," Joe said, looking at Frank for help or support or *anything*, "we hoped to see, um, Monsieur Berot—"

The young woman shook her head, checking a large appointment book on the desk. "I'm sorry, but I don't have an appointment listed for you. And on weekends—"

Her hand went to a phone, but then Joe started shaking his head. "No, no, that's okay. I'll, uh, talk with him early next week."

He slunk off toward the exit, with Frank trailing behind. As Joe opened the door, however, he stopped for a second, looking back. "Um, I hope you have a nice time at the party."

The girl looked back with a totally straight face. "Thank you."

Joe slouched out, with Frank in hot pursuit, shaking his head. "How could you make such a stupid spectacle—" he hissed.

His words were drowned out as soon as the door closed—by Joe's laughter.

Reaching into his jacket, Joe pulled out two gleaming white parchment envelopes.

"The spectacle worked, big brother. We've got our invitations to what may be the theft of the century."

Chapter

15

"I FEEL LIKE AN IDIOT," Joe whispered. The cab he was riding in stopped short, and for about the fifteenth time that evening, he was jabbed in the ribs by his own sword.

It was supposed to hang beside his hip from a sash. It completed the outfit of his Continental Army officer's uniform. But in the cramped confines of the cab, it turned into a dangerous item every time they hit a bump.

Frank Hardy smoothed down the lace of his Virginia planter's outfit. "Calm down, Joe. You'll look fine when we get there."

"Right," Callie added, struggling with her own costume. "At least you don't have to worry about these stupid hoops sending your skirt flying up whenever you sit down."

"I'm just glad we get to wear masks," Joe complained. "Did you see the looks we were getting in the hotel?"

"That's just because we got into a cab instead of a limousine," Callie said. "It looks like everybody who's anybody knows about this costume ball."

"We should be glad we found costumes today," Frank said.

"Right," said Joe as the cab stopped and he got jabbed again. "Glad."

The cab left the expressway and began driving along the wandering roads that bounded Rock Creek Park.

"This is a nice neighborhood," Callie said, looking out the window at tree-covered estates hiding mansions.

"It ought to be," said Frank, who had spent the afternoon reading his guidebook. "The Vice President's house is around here—and so is the Russian Embassy."

"How fascinating," Joe told his brother. "How about the place we're heading?"

"It's an old mansion overlooking Rock Creek, which the last owner deeded to the Continental Order."

"And what's this order?" Callie wanted to know.

"It's sort of a veterans association, founded by the officers in the Continental Army," Frank said. "About two thousand four hundred men joined after the Revolutionary War. Membership passes down through each family to the oldest living son descended from the original officer."

"What about the house?" Joe prompted.

"There's a ballroom on the ground floor—that's where the party will take place," Frank went on. "The museum is on the second floor. It's full of paintings and memorabilia from the Revolution. That's where the sword will probably wind up." He looked at the other two. "You understand what our jobs are?"

Joe nodded. "I'll keep an eye on the Berots and try to keep them from getting near the sword." He gave his brother a hard look. "I mean, we are assuming this guy is here to steal the sword."

Frank shrugged. "It's something beyond price for a collector. And a mad collector is the only kind of person I can imagine paying the freight for the kind of operation we've stumbled onto."

"Anyway, you guys will be trying to get ahold of Maddy—I mean, Nadine," Joe went on, looking at Frank and Callie. "I hope you have better luck than I did, finding out where the real Berots are."

Callie smiled grimly. "Don't worry. After all she's pulled on me, I'll be happy to talk to her."

The cab passed an old-fashioned graveyard,

then pulled up to an iron gate. Security guards checked their invitations, then waved them in.

Frank paid the fare and adjusted his mask. "Well, we're in."

"I still feel stupid," Joe groused, setting his sash and his sword by his hip.

"Better smarten up quick," Callie advised, "before we start tangling with these thieves."

They stepped into the mansion and followed the sound of music to the ballroom. Spacious halls decorated with colonial flags and statues of Revolutionary War heroes led them into a vaulted room at least thirty feet high. A spectacular staircase led up to a musicians' gallery—that was where the music came from.

The ballroom looked like the set from an elaborate historical movie. Hundreds of people were standing around in colonial garb. Men in silks and satins, wearing powdered wigs, talked and danced with women in lace gowns, elaborate hairdos, and glittering jewels.

"We shouldn't feel stupid," Callie whispered, trying not to stare. "I think we should feel tacky."

"Forget about that," Joe said, adjusting his mask as they started circulating through the crowd. "We've got to find the Berots."

"There—by the entrance," Frank suddenly said.

Three people had just come in—a tall, thin,

hawk-faced man in a white uniform, a middle-aged woman in a dazzling gown, and a younger woman in a simple blue gown and a white-powdered wig with ringlets. All of them wore masks.

"We didn't plan on recognizing them in costumes," Callie said. "But I think those are the people we want. Look at the widow's peak on the man."

The woman scanned the growing crowd and rubbed her hands nervously.

"That's her little gesture. I saw her do that all the time I was following her yesterday. They're *definitely* the phony Berots," Callie said. "Now let's see if we can talk to Nadine."

Joe, Frank, and Callie started across the room, making their way around flouncing skirts and dress swords that stuck out at just the right height to trip them.

The swirling crowd hid them until they were almost on top of the false Berots. Then, as luck would have it, the glittering mob parted—and Nadine saw them coming.

Apparently, their costumes weren't as good as some of the others, because Nadine recognized them right away. Her face went pale as she turned to her supposed parents and excused herself. Then she dashed out the door.

The Hardys and Callie reached the double doors that led to the ballroom and saw Nadine trying to get down the now crowded hallway. It wasn't easy in the wide gown she wore. She glanced desperately over her shoulder as they came closer, then scuttled down a short flight of stairs. She ran down another hall, made for a door, went through, and slammed it in their faces.

Frank and Joe halted. " 'Ladies,' " Frank read. "We can't chase her in there."

Callie's hands balled into fists. "I can."

She burst through the door, giving the Hardys a momentary glimpse of a lavish pink and green interior. The door closed, and immediately after came some very unladylike shrieks—thankfully muffled by the thick walls. Then came a couple of loud thumps. Frank and Joe studied the ceiling, feeling very conspicuous.

The door opened to reveal a somewhat bedraggled Nadine. Her powdered wig was slanted at a strange angle, and two of the ringlets now hung in her face. Callie sailed along behind her, with a satisfied smile on her face. "Here we are, back again," she said as if nothing had happened.

"I was a little worried for you, Callie," Frank said, moving to make sure Nadine didn't try another run for it.

Callie's smile got bigger. "Let's just say Nadine was the one you should have worried about."

With her back to a marble wall and the three American kids surrounding her, Nadine wilted. "Okay, I found out what you wanted to know.

The real Berots are being held in a bad part of town." She rattled off an address. "The theft is supposed to happen tonight, but I still don't know what's supposed to be stolen." She bit her lip. "It's getting scary, guys. I think La Bête was talking to Paul about getting rid of me afterward— one less to worry about in the getaway. The guy is crazy."

Frank repeated the address to Nadine, who nodded. "Down in the southeast area. We'd better get going." He grabbed Nadine's hand and put it into Joe's. "You'll have to keep Nadine here—and keep an eye on the fake Mr. Berot," he said. "We're off on a rescue mission."

"But first," Callie said with a grin, "a moment for fashion." She took hold of the wig on Nadine's head and twisted it so it sat the way it should. "Much better," she said. Then she and Frank hustled for the exit.

They were lucky enough to hail a cab that was dropping off another couple. The driver gave them a surprised look when they gave him the address.

"You want to go there—looking like *that?*" the man said, staring at their costumes.

"We don't have a choice," Frank told the man. "It's a matter of life and death."

Looking very doubtful, the driver set off.

Frank could understand the guy's doubts when they reached their destination. It was a large, dilapidated building that hadn't seen fresh paint or a clean-up crew in years.

"Only warehouses around here," the driver said. "You sure you got the right address?"

"I'm pretty sure," Frank said, looking around the deserted streets. "We're supposed to find some people here and bring them back to the party. Look, can I pay you something extra to ask you to stick around? I think it will be hard to get another cab in this neighborhood."

"Hard?" the driver said. "Try impossible." He shook his head. "This isn't a place where I'd like to hang out."

"Please?" Callie said. "What we're doing is very important—if it works out, we've got to get right back where we came from."

"All right." The driver shrugged. "I'll wait a couple of minutes."

Looking like ghosts from another era, Frank and Callie ran for the warehouse door. "Locked," Frank reported, looking at the rusted steel gate that blocked their entrance.

"What a surprise in this neighborhood," Callie said. "So how do we get in?"

Frank scanned the front of the building. "Wait a second. The gate on that loading dock isn't pulled down all the way."

They climbed to the top of the dock and examined the door. "I think I can slip through under there," Frank said.

130

"But there's no way I can fit under there," Callie said, shaking her huge skirt.

"I'll go in and check the place out—if there's no guard, I'll open the door."

Callie didn't look happy, but she didn't have a choice. "Okay," she finally said. "But be careful." She tried to smile at him. "Remember, we've got big deposits on these costumes."

"I'll try not to get mine dirty." Frank gave her a quick kiss. Then he slid through the opening under the door, blinking in the darkness of the warehouse interior. Slowly, he could make out enormous rows of shelves with empty alleys between them. He also realized that there was a very faint light off in one corner of the warehouse.

He was making his way to the source of the ghostly glow when he became aware of a sound behind him. Whipping around, he realized it was the sound of footsteps—heading away from him, back toward the loading bay door!

Apparently the thugs had left a guard, who was now making his rounds!

Silently the automatic door began to rise. Frank took off for the guard as fast as he could.

The guard was standing peering out at the dark loading dock, a pistol in one hand. He switched on the flashlight he held in the other.

Pinned in the beam of the guard's light, like a giant moth, was the white-gowned Callie Shaw.

Chapter

16

FOR A LONG MOMENT the guard with the light and Callie just stared at each other, each equally astonished.

That was all the time Frank Hardy needed.

He launched himself at the guard's back, crashing into him, bringing the man down before he could even raise his gun. The pistol the guy had been carrying clattered off somewhere in the darkness, while his flashlight skittered off in the opposite direction.

In spite of his surprise, the guard reacted quickly to Frank's attack. He squirmed out from under the attacking Hardy, rolled onto his back, and aimed a devastating kick at Frank's face.

The kick whipped right under Frank's nose as

he pulled back. It was so close, Frank could feel the wind from its passing.

They both got to their feet now, and the guard snapped a kick at Frank's stomach. Frank blocked it with his forearm and aimed one of his own at the guy's hip.

The guard nimbly stepped aside and swept Frank's legs from under him with a roundhouse kick. Frank got to his knees, but he was knocked flat on his back again when the guard's foot caught him on the chin.

Frank lay stunned as the man moved in for the kill.

The next thing he knew, the guy was crumpling to the floor.

"How—" Frank began. Then he saw Callie standing over him, the now-flickering flashlight in her hand.

"I hope this thing will still work," she said, jiggling the switch. "Maybe I broke it when I hit that guy over the head."

Frank unbuckled the guard's belt and used it to tie the man's wrists together. His tie was used on his feet. Then Frank and Callie explored the warehouse. There were no more guards, but in the corner of the place, they found an old sign that read Secure Storage Area.

The area didn't look all that secure. There was a simple cyclone fence blocking off one corner. But it was obviously secure enough to hold prisoners. Handcuffed to a set of metal shelves were three people—a tall, hawk-faced man, a pretty blond woman, and a cute teenage girl. The real Berots were not identical to the impostors, but they looked enough alike for Frank to feel an eerie chill.

Mr. Berot shouted at them in French, but it was Maddy whose eyes went wide. "C-Callie?" she said in disbelief.

"We found out what was going on, and now we've found you," Callie said, trying to open the lock on the gate in the fence. "We'll get you out."

The overhead lights suddenly flashed on, blinding them all temporarily, and a voice behind them said, "I do not think so."

Frank and Callie whirled around to find themselves staring down the muzzle of a 9mm pistol. Beyond that, they recognized the lumpy face of La Bête.

"That Georges, he is not a good guard," the big man said, shaking his head. "The others and I, we go to the cemetery to get ready for the getaway. But when I look from behind the gravestone, I see you two coming away. So I follow and find you here."

"You saw what went on with the guard? Why didn't you step in then?" Frank asked.

"I arrive just too late," La Bête said, coming a little closer, lining them both up under his gun.

"Then I decide it is better if I let you come deep inside, where things will be quiet."

He smiled at them, revealing stained teeth. "I have to kill these ones," he said, indicating the Berots. "And you make my job so much easier by coming here—"

His words cut off in a choke as Frank's hand shot up to release a cloud of orange powder in La Bête's face. Frank's other hand jarred into Callie, knocking her aside as the French thug, eyes streaming, triggered a blind shot into the area where they'd been standing.

Frank swung around La Bête, smashing karate blows into the thug's shoulders and neck. The man was strong—he took a lot of punishment—but finally Frank managed to floor him. The gun skittered away and Frank knocked him unconscious.

"What was that orange powder bit?" Callie said while Frank tied the thug up.

"Cayenne pepper," Frank answered with a smile. "I picked some up this afternoon while we were out costume hunting. Why not take a page from this guy's book and have a secret weapon on hand?"

"Well, it certainly worked," Callie said, watching La Bête blink in pain. "Hey, look what I found." She opened the desk drawer and came out with a ring of keys. "I think I know where these go."

Sure enough, the keys worked on the lock on the gate and on the handcuffs that held the Berots prisoner.

"We can put La Bête and Georges in here for safekeeping, then call the cops," Frank said. "I think their little scheme has just fallen apart." He quickly located a phone.

Through the glittering whirl of the costume party, Joe Hardy was moving across the ballroom floor, toward the stairway to the musicians' balcony. He tightened his grip on Nadine's wrist. "I think your pal is making his move," he whispered. "Why is he going up there?"

"What?" Nadine's head spun around from where she'd been eyeing somebody's jewelry. Joe was glad he'd kept at least one of her hands out of action.

"Paul is going up the stairs to the orchestra. The question is, why?"

High above them, the disguised thief handed some papers to the bandleader and chatted with him for a moment.

Instead of coming down from the music gallery, the Frenchman headed past the band. Reaching the door behind the musicians, he exited through it.

"Come on—we've got to catch up with him." Still holding on to Nadine's wrist, Joe led the way to the stairs. When she jerked to a stop behind him, he was almost pulled off his feet. "What?" he said.

Then he saw the reason Nadine had stopped. Standing at the foot of the stairway, guarding it, he decided, was the false Mrs. Berot—Paul's accomplice, Sylvie.

The woman looked from Nadine to Joe, and her face went cold.

Now Nadine was pulling Joe away. "I'm dead, I'm dead," she moaned. "She saw me with you, recognized you. They probably think I brought you here. They're going to kill me."

Joe swung the girl around to face him. "Look, this place is crawling with cops and security guards. We can go to them and stop this heist right now." She shook her head, cringing. "Then my only hope is to stop Paul from stealing that sword myself." He took charge now, heading for the ballroom entrance.

"I'm going upstairs to check out the museum."

Nadine stopped again. "Not me," she said decisively. "And I don't want to be left alone."

"How am I supposed—" Then Joe saw another familiar face. "Ansel, my man," he said brightly, grabbing the German kid's arm. "Glad you could make it."

Ansel's eyes went wide as he realized who was speaking to him.

"Hey, I want you to have a good time," Joe said. "Why don't you dance with Maddy here?"

He put Nadine's hand in Ansel's. "Rob him blind," he whispered in Nadine's ear.

Joe rushed from the ballroom and headed for the main staircase. He ran up the stairs and to the closed front door, but the door wasn't locked.

Pushing it open, Joe headed down a long hall lined with portraits of military and political leaders from the days of the Revolution. Glass display cases lined the walls as well, filled with medals, buttons, snuffboxes, and weapons from the War for Independence.

At the end of the hall Joe spotted a hint of movement—a shadow flitting around in the deeper darkness of the dimly lit museum.

Joe reached the end of the hall just as the white-clad figure lifted something from a display case.

"Paul," Joe called, "you can't get away with taking the Lafayette sword."

The thief whirled around, a jeweled sword and scabbard in his hands. "You!" he gasped. "What are you doing here?"

"I'm here to stop you from stealing that sword," Joe told him. "It's the least I can do to pay you and your pals back for trying to kill me." He gestured to the sword. "How do you expect to get that out of here, anyway?"

Paul gestured to the scabbard and sword he

was wearing with his costume. "I'll just make a substitution. My fake sword for this real one."

He slipped the Lafayette sword from the scabbard and stalked toward Joe, holding the blade at chest level.

"And believe me, this is a real sword."

Chapter

17

"I'LL GIVE YOU one final lesson in history," the thief said, moving on Joe like a bullfighter. "This is called a smallsword."

To Joe, the three-foot blade looked large enough.

"It's quite famous in the history of weapons," Paul went on, flicking the sword at Joe's eyes. "In its day, it killed more people than any other class of weapon. And it held the record until the invention of the machine gun."

"How endlessly fascinating," Joe said, backing down the hall. "And how did you find that out?"

"Research," Paul replied, matching Joe step for step. "In my business, you do quite a lot of research."

Keeping his eyes fixed on the point of the

blade, Joe tried to remember how many steps he'd taken to get from the door and staircase to where Paul was stealing the Lafayette sword.

Paul seemed to read his mind. "You're too far from the stairs to run or call for help," he said. "Besides, you'd have to turn your back on me to run." He flicked out the blade again, and Joe flinched back. "I don't think that would be a good idea."

A smile flitted over Paul's hatchet face, as if Joe amused him. "Besides, a fine, upstanding American like you would surely rather face death than take it in the back."

The smile disappeared—Paul was finished playing. He launched himself at Joe in an overhand thrust, aiming straight for Joe's heart.

Joe twisted aside, trying to pull the sword from his own scabbard to defend himself. No sword came out. The hilt and the scabbard were all one, a useless prop.

Paul's sword was far from useless. Although the thrust missed, the sharpened tip of the small sword sliced right through Joe's costume sash, releasing Joe's scabbard. The Lafayette sword may never have been used, but it had been kept razor-sharp.

At least Joe now had his phony sword free to parry Paul's thrusts. Two pieces of sash material flapped from it as he desperately warded off Paul's attacks.

Joe retreated down the hallway, managing to knock Paul's sword thrusts off-target. It wasn't easy, since the sword's point circled wickedly in front of him, threatening him from all possible angles.

Don't pay attention to the sword, Joe ordered himself. Pay attention to the guy's eyes. He managed to keep the plastic prop between him and death, but he didn't know how much longer the game could go on. The hallway restricted his field of action, and sooner or later Paul would send a thrust home.

Paul stopped stabbing with the sword and began slashing with it, taking nicks of plastic out of Joe's defense.

Joe just managed to leap back as the Lafayette blade sliced through the arm and half the front of his uniform coat. The coat gaped open, almost torn in two.

I'm going to have a tough time explaining this to the costume rental place, Joe thought. He ducked as the sword whistled over his head. That's the least of my problems right now, though.

Frank, Callie, and the Berots sat in tense silence as the cab driver roared straight for the mansion headquarters of the Continental Order. "Have the police arrived?" Frank asked the uniformed guard who stopped them to check their invitations.

A familiar figure stepped out of the shadows of the gate house—Lieutenant Grant. He wore another expensive suit and a dubious frown. "We've been here all night, Mr. Hardy. One of my people gave me a radio report that there was supposed to be a robbery going down. I decided to wait and check you out first. After all, you had some connection with the Berot girl's shoplifting attempt."

"That wasn't the real Madeleine Berot," Callie said, pointing to the people in the backseat of the cab. "*This* is the real Maddy—and this is her real mother and father."

"You've got a couple of impostors inside that headquarters building," Frank explained, "and a bunch of French thugs hiding next door in that graveyard."

Throughout this whole report, Grant's frown only deepened. "I think we'd better check out that museum upstairs," he said. "Then we'll worry about the graveyard."

Frank was with the first wave of plainclothes police to surge up the main stairway. When they reached the top, they all stopped in surprise, staring at a scene that looked like something out of an old movie.

Paul, in his gleaming white uniform, aimed slash after slash at Joe Hardy, whose costume

THE HARDY BOYS CASEFILES

now looked like a collection of tatters. The tip of his prop scabbard had been cut off, and it looked as if his ragged uniform coat were about to fall off, too.

As the police officers came charging up, Joe glanced back at his brother. "About time you guys showed up," he growled.

Joe had to give Paul credit for one thing—a lot of nerve. "I found this boy trying to break into the case to steal the Lafayette sword." He looked at the sea of police facing him and recognized Lieutenant Grant. "You know me, I'm Henri Berot, and the sword is my responsibility."

"Still trying to ruin people's reputations, are you?" Frank asked. "It won't wash this time, Paul. You see, the cops have already caught La Bête."

That jarred Paul badly, but he still kept up his act. "What is the word of a French criminal against that of an accredited diplomat? I still claim diplomatic immunity."

"No, you do not."

The real Henri Berot came out of the crowd. "That man is an impostor and a kidnapper. I demand that he be taken into custody, pending final proof of our identities from Paris."

"You cannot arrest me," Paul bluffed.

"Oh, we can," Lieutenant Grant assured him. "This isn't the French embassy, so we lowly D.C. police types have jurisdiction here. If you'll put down that piece of evidence you're hold-ing—''

"No!" Paul suddenly brought the tip of his sword in contact with Joe's chest. "If you make a move toward me, I'll run him through.''

Lots of pistols were aimed at Paul, but none went off. Joe realized that police regulations were as good as a bulletproof vest for the thief. As long as Joe was in the line of fire, none of the cops could shoot.

"Great," he said. "First this clown ruins my clothes. Now he's going to fill me with steel.''

Joe shrugged, and his coat started falling off his shoulders. That's what he'd planned on. Dodging to one side, he flung the tattered cos-tume into Paul's face.

Paul recovered quickly. He couldn't bring his entangled sword around, but when Joe tried to grapple with him, he straight-armed the younger Hardy.

Joe toppled back into the crowd of police, blocking their guns and their rush for a critical instant.

Paul took that instant to sprint down the hall-way, sword still in hand, and smash through a closed window.

Burglar alarms began to clamor wildly, but the secret was out now. So was the priceless sword, still in Paul's grasp.

Lieutenant Grant led the police charge down

the hall and leaned out the window, checking out the ground below. "Where'd he go?" the lieutenant asked. "He's not down there."

Joe leaned out the window, a grim look on his face. "If he didn't go down, then he went up."

Digging his fingertips into the elaborate stone carvings around the windowsill, he began climbing up the face of the building. From the tip of the windowsill cornice, he discovered it was an easy stretch to reach the roof. "Come on, guys, you can climb right up," he called down to the others below.

He hesitated for a second at the low fence that surrounded the roof. He didn't want Paul to catch him half over the white stone railing—not when a well-placed kick could send him falling three stories.

Paul wasn't anywhere to be seen. Joe swung up and over. In the distance, he saw Paul legging it, taking a diagonal course across the graveled roof.

"Joe," a panting voice called from behind him. "Wait up for the reinforcements."

He glanced back to see Frank pull himself up. He'd gotten rid of his fancy jacket and shirt, wearing just a T-shirt and the costume pants.

Joe didn't even comment on how ridiculous his brother looked. He tore off in pursuit of the fleeing thief.

Paul was still carrying the Lafayette sword,

holding it over his head as he ran. He looked as if he were leading a charge. In this case, however, the troops were the police, who had just climbed the wall, and Frank and Joe Hardy.

A deep indentation—perhaps an air shaft—cut into the roof, separating one wing of the mansion from the rest of the building.

Hearing the noise behind him, Paul didn't even glance back. Increasing his speed, he thrust one foot to the top of the railing and jumped the empty space.

He almost made it.

Maybe if Paul had had both hands free, he'd have been able to grab the white stone railing. Instead, he landed, toppled, then slid down the face of the balustrade, frantically holding on with one hand to a small stone pillar.

"The guy's a goner," Joe heard one of the police officers say behind him.

He picked up his feet, taking the last few yards of the roof at top speed. "*Joe!*" He heard Frank's horrified yell behind him—Callie's, too. Somehow she'd also made it onto the roof.

Then he had no time to pay attention to anything. He was leaping into thin air.

The balustrade on the far roof came at Joe much faster than he expected. Still, he managed to grab it two-handed and swing himself over.

Joe moved along the railing until he reached

the spot where Paul was dangling, the Lafayette sword still clutched in his free hand.

"Don't be stupid, Paul. Pass up the sword, then I'll help you onto the roof."

Paul snarled, realizing his situation was hopeless. Finally he flung the sword at Joe. A moment later Joe returned the compliment, dragging Paul over the railing and flinging him to the roof. He had the thief in a half nelson by the time the police caught up with them.

While that little drama was being played out, the sound of sirens cut the air as police cruisers converged on the nearby graveyard. A fast car hidden behind a mausoleum threw up a shower of gravel as it tried to make an escape, but the road out of the cemetery was blocked.

Lieutenant Grant was smiling by the time Joe was back indoors again. "We caught three guys in the graveyard, yelling in French to one another," he said to Frank. "That's in addition to the two you left locked up in the warehouse—and the one *you* just tackled," he added, turning to Joe.

"Lieutenant," one of the plainclothes detectives called, coming up to make a report. "We've got the other two accomplices downstairs in the ballroom."

Police officers brought up a furious Sylvie, spitting French as she struggled against her handcuffs.

"What's she saying?" Joe asked Callie.

"I can guess," she told him with a smile, "but I wouldn't know the idioms."

The police also brought up a scared-looking Nadine.

"Something a little more serious than shoplifting this time," Lieutenant Grant told her grimly. "And this time there's no phony diplomatic immunity." He shook his head. "It's like I always say—petty infractions lead to worse crimes."

"Uh, Lieutenant," Joe said, stepping over to the police officer. "Don't be hard on her. Without her help, we'd never have been able to save the Berots."

Nadine's face was white, but her voice was calm as she spoke to Lieutenant Grant. "Sir, I will tell you everything I know about this plot."

Lieutenant Grant smiled at the girl and nodded. "In view of her cooperation, perhaps she could get off lightly," he said. "She just might."

"Well, it looks like we've tied everything up," Joe said to Callie and Frank. "The Lafayette sword is safe, Paul the thief is captured, his strong-arm man is in jail—"

"And the girl who got me in trouble with the cops is facing a lot worse than I ever got," Callie chimed in, grinning. "Even if you turned out to be soft on her."

"Me? Soft?" Joe protested. "She did help us, after all."

149

"Right. All we had to do was back her into a corner and threaten to punch her head in," Callie shot back.

Frank sighed. "The situation must be normal. You two are fighting like cats and dogs again."

He nudged Callie, nodding down the hallway. "Do you think you can knock it off for a couple of minutes, though? Your French friends are coming this way."

The real Berot family came up to Frank, Joe, and Callie, looking a little embarrassed. "We didn't have a chance to thank you properly for rescuing us," Mr. Berot said. Even in a torn suit and with unshaven stubble on his face, he was every inch the distinguished diplomat. "You saved our lives, and you saved the Lafayette sword. My family and I will always be in your debt."

He smiled and said, "If what I heard from the police is a sample, the impostors did not show you much hospitality. We, at least, hope to make up for that by showing you a good time for the rest of your visit."

"Yes, *indeed*," Madeleine said, stepping up to take Frank's arm. "Callie often wrote to me about the adventures of her friends the Hardys. But I never expected to see you in action. My hero," she said, flashing him a smile even brighter than Nadine's best efforts. "So brave—and so *handsome*. You never told me that, Callie."

"Well, Maddy," said Callie, taking Frank's other arm, "some things are best not shared."

They marched off with a very nervous-looking Frank between them.

Joe followed them, shaking his head. "Oh, boy," he muttered. "This is going to be some vacation."

Frank and Joe's next case:

A tornado has hit Bayport, but the deadliest storm is still brewing—in the Hardy home. Years ago, Fenton Hardy sent a criminal named Leonard Mock to prison. Now Mock's son has returned to Bayport to seek revenge. He has vowed to put Frank and Joe's father away for good!

But Leonard Mock lost his son to adoption when the boy was five. His name was changed, and the only clue to his identity is that he has since befriended the Hardy boys! Then the brothers uncover a shocking and horrifying piece of evidence. The person out to murder their father may very well be none other than Chet Morton—their best and most trusted friend . . . in *Flesh and Blood*, Case #39 in The Hardy Boys Casefiles™.